# The Wrong Turn

# NC Marshall

The Wrong Turn
Copyright © NC Marshall 2017

# Prologue

I'm cursed! The two words play out over and over again in my head, and even though I have never believed in that sort of mumbo jumbo, it's the only explanation that makes any sense as to why this could be happening right now. Or, maybe I did something wrong in a previous life? After a year or more of constant heartache and pain, one thing after another thrown at me, and now, as the brakes in my car refuse to slow me down, my conclusion is – I am cursed!

The car ahead, which has veered onto the wrong side of the road, continues to hurtle towards me. Its headlights flash, dazzling me, and causing temporary loss of sight. I continue to frantically pump my foot on the brake pedal. Nothing!

Before I know it, I hit the bridge. The other car continues to speed towards me and no attempt is being made to slow it down. I continue to work the brake pedal, again with no response. Now, the approaching car is directly ahead, meeting me at the centre of the deserted bridge. There's not enough room to pass on the narrow road, and I know I'm travelling far too quickly, but I have no choice other than to attempt the tricky manoeuvre and avoid a potentially fatal head-on collision.

Turning the steering wheel sharply, just before impact, the other car clips mine and I immediately lose control. I swerve hazardously off the road, through the barrier, and down into the forested area that surrounds us. I've driven along this road numerous times and know the area like the back of my hand, but I hadn't realized that there was such a steep decline. As the car accelerates, I catch sight of the vehicle that has succeeded in forcing me off the road, its tail lights disappearing into the darkness through my rearview mirror.

My car now moves even faster, plummeting down further into the overgrown ravine. Tree branches bang against the windscreen, scraping and scratching at the glass. I grip the steering wheel as tightly as I can and pray that I will survive, but when my car hits something solid and is thrown violently to one side, I only feel despair.

There's a loud bang as the car rolls, and I'm jolted in all directions as it flies into the air and hits the ground with a deafening thud. There's a loud bang that accompanies it, and I connect with the airbag, which has now inflated. A shattering sound follows and I scream out as the windscreen implodes and I'm showered with glass. A sharp pain drives across my temple and the strong metallic taste of blood floods my mouth. As the relentless groaning of crumpling metal continues, I close my eyes.

When I finally find the courage to open them, the car has stopped moving and I'm aware that I'm upside down. Touching my temple gingerly, I can feel a warm, sticky trickle of blood; still, I don't feel any pain.

An icy wind is gushing around me and my small car is now barely recognizable – nothing more than a piece of tangled scrap metal. Crisp autumn leaves are scattered across the inside of the wreckage.

The car has finally settled at the bottom of the ravine and although its pitch black, the headlights and soft glow of the moon allow me to get my bearings. I try to move, but I'm pinned back by my seatbelt and my legs are trapped under the twisted steering column. I search around, desperately trying to think of a way I can escape the wreckage, but my vision is blurred and my mind is disorientated and confused.

I focus on breathing and inhale deeply, trying to stop the shaking of my entire body. The stench of exhaust fumes and petrol saturates the early evening forest air, and sparks dance from the now-visible electric wires of the dashboard, hanging to my side.

"Help me!" I shout, desperately, and my voice echoes back from beyond the trees. "Please – someone help me!" I hear nothing more than the deafening quiet of the dense surrounding woodland.

"Someone, please!" I scream again, as loudly as I can through excruciating sobs of fear.

I wriggle in my seat and, with every ounce of strength I have left, I try to force my legs out, but it's no good, I'm tightly trapped. Prior to this, I've not believed in God, but I begin to chant a prayer, begging him to get me through this and spare my life. However, it seems that tonight, even God isn't listening!

Attempting to calm down, I try and focus on a way of escaping, but when a large electrical spark flashes to the left of me, causing a small fire to ignite outside the car, I begin to lose control.

"Help, please someone help me!" I scream frantically into the night and, although I thrash back and forth, trying to free myself, the seatbelt's grip doesn't budge. The flames flicker nearer to me, setting alight the dry heaps of leaves on the ground, and edging forward, they begin licking hungrily at the body of the wreckage.

The heat is already so intense that I can barely breathe, and every inhalation I do manage makes my lungs burn.

*I'm going to die! Right here, right now, I'm going to die!*

I continue to struggle – I can't give up. I've gone through too much lately to lose my life in this way, but as the heat becomes more unbearable, and the flames crawl nearer, I know I have no choice but to surrender.

Minutes go by, or maybe only seconds and I close my eyes and welcome the darkness, knowing it's time to let go. Salty tears slipping down my cheeks sting my dry lips. I'm losing consciousness and, as I can feel myself slipping into the comfort of sleep, I hear a sound close by, causing me to snap back to a state of semi-awareness. It's the sound of dried leaves crunching, and it's getting closer. Footsteps! *There's someone here*!

"Help me, please help me," I plead again, but my voice is barely a croaky whisper, silent to anyone but myself.

"Hey, it's OK, you're going to be alright," I hear a distant voice reply. *Thank you, God*!

I frantically search for the owner of the voice, but it's too dark to see properly. Suddenly my door is wrenched open and I catch a glimpse of feet, and then a blistered hand reaches over to untangle me from my twisted seatbelt. I try to control my coughing as I feel an arm wrap around me, and I am torn from the driver's seat so that my legs are finally free.

 My head swims, shadows and blurred shapes dance in front of my eyes. We stagger a short distance when I'm lowered gently to the forest floor, landing in a heap and unable to sit upright. I can smell the earth beneath me and feel the cold mud against the back of my sweltering neck. A cluster of leaves catches on the breeze, and blow through my hair. As I start to lose consciousness again, I dig my fingernails into the ground and force myself to stay awake; I then feel something similar to a blanket being placed over me.

I'm moving now, quickly, further away from the car, and my rescuer has me in their arms. I peer behind us where the sky is alive with a bright orange glow, and I can feel the breeze against my face, icy against the hot and damp streaks of blood, sweat and tears. As we continue up the hill, I break down and bury my head into the shoulder of my lifesaver. We are almost back to the road above when the car behind us explodes with an almighty bang.

# Chapter 1

"Well, look who's awake!"

My eyelids flicker open and I squint against the blinding light that stings my gritty eyes. With my right hand up to my face, I try to shift from the rays blazing through a small window to my side.

"Try not to move, darling. You've been through a bit of an ordeal."

I attempt to sit upright as a plastic beaker of water is thrust into my hand and, accepting it, I take a sip – it instantly soothes my burning throat. My dad's face comes into focus as he fusses with the corner of the white sheet covering me.

"Where am I?" I ask. My voice is deep and scratchy, nowhere close to its normal sound.

"You're in hospital, love," my dad replies soothingly.

"Why, what happened to me?" I touch my eyebrow, which seems to have been bandaged, and I feel an instant stabbing sensation across my forehead. I wince with pain and drag myself into a sitting position.

"You were in an accident, but you're safe now." My dad rubs my shoulder.

"What accident?" I ask him, with no recollection whatsoever.

"Don't you remember, Megan? You were in a car accident last night." My brother Luke's voice emerges into the bright room before he appears on the opposite side of the bed to my dad. "Your car came off the road down at Kitley Bridge."

"Oh my God," I reply, as I'm hit with a flashback. I put a hand across my stomach, suddenly feeling nauseous.

"The doctor says you're going to be fine, love. You have a cut to your head and a few nasty grazes, but apart from that you are OK, thank goodness." My dad takes my cup and refills it from a large plastic jug on the bedside cabinet.

"Can you remember what happened, Meg?" asks Luke. He sits down gently at the bottom of the bed and I study his face. The usually perfectly groomed hair and carefree expression he wears has been replaced by a disheveled and tired-looking appearance; he seems to have aged 10 years since I last saw him about 48 hours ago.

"I think so," I reply, fighting images of being pulled from the car and gripping someone's neck as they carried me back up to the bridge.

"Someone pulled me from the car," I say.

"Yeah, the nurse told us someone rescued you," replies Luke, before glancing again at our dad, who is still fussing around me. Although they are doing a great job of trying to mask it, both men have a concerned look on their faces, which reveals their true emotions.

"I'm so glad someone saw you down there," adds my dad. "If it hadn't been for them, I can't bring myself to think what could have happened to you." He pauses to look down at me and bites his lower lip. Dark circles shadow his kind, green eyes and his skin is pale – he too looks absolutely shattered.

"Is the person who saved me still here?" I ask hopefully. "I'd really like to thank them."

"No," says my dad. Finally, he stops fussing and sits down on a chair next to me. "You've been asleep all night, Meg. It was just some bloke who was passing by; he called an ambulance at the roadside and made sure you were attended to, but didn't come with you to the hospital."

"Your purse was in the pocket of your jeans, so the hospital staff were able to identify you and call us," adds Luke.

"I'd just been to buy petrol – I'd stayed late at the office and was on my way home," I offer, trying to ignore the overpowering smell of leaking fuel that seems embedded in my nostrils.

Luke nods and gives my dad another worrying glance.

"Do you know who it was?" I ask.

"Who?"

"The man who saved me." I focus my attention on my brother, then shift my weight on the bed as pain shoots down the length of my left leg. I wriggle it under the covers to try and dull the discomfort.

"I've spoken to the paramedics who dealt with you last night," answers Luke. "They had to rush you here and they didn't get a name from the guy."

"You were lucky he was passing on that bridge and saw your car at the bottom of the ravine," adds Dad.

"I would like to have said thank you," I whisper back thoughtfully. I turn to look out of the hospital window, now able to stand the light coming through, which isn't as bright as I had first thought. The weak morning sun filters through the orange leaves on the trees, leaving a pattern on the empty hospital grounds outside. In normal circumstances I would appreciate the view – the perfect example of an autumnal day. Today, however, it only makes me more aware of where I am, and why I am here.

"The police have already been down to where the crash happened," says Luke. My dad shoots him a glance as if to tell him to be quiet, but I urge my brother to continue.

"Why are the police involved? Did you call them?" I ask.

"Well, no, you…" Luke begins to stammer.

"Come on, Luke, spit it out!"

"You told the paramedics that you were run off the road." Luke finally admits. My dad rolls his eyes at my brother.

As soon as Luke says these words, another powerful flashback hits me − a car's lights hurtling towards me at an unforgiving speed and then the sickening rear view of it driving off into the darkness, leaving me for dead.

"We weren't going to mention anything to you just yet, about the other car and the police. You need to get yourself better, Meg and you don't need any added stress right now," orders my dad.

"No, Dad, it's alright, honest. I'm sure it would have come back to me at some point anyway." I wave my hand to silence my dad before he has chance to speak again. "Do they know who was driving the other car?" I ask Luke.

"They think it was kids, but they're still looking into it," he answers. "They told us that they'll have to speak to you."

I nod as a young nurse enters the ward and stops at the bottom of my bed, next to Luke. She looks down at him and flushes slightly when he notices her, before bending over to pick up a clipboard and study it. Luke catches my eye and flashes me a cheeky grin before he checks out her backside and moves out of her way.

"How are you feeling Mrs Cooper?" she asks, flashing my brother another quick glance through her thick lashes.

My dad shakes his head in disapproval. My younger brother has been a flirt since his late teens and, at the age of almost 28, I have no hope that he's about to change his ways any time soon.

I regain the nurse's attention and smile, preparing myself for an Oscar-winning performance.

"Quite good, considering," I answer brightly. I actually feel pretty dreadful, but my dad doesn't need to know that, and I also want to get out of here as soon as possible.

"You were very lucky." The nurse smiles back at me and reaches to adjust the dressing above my eye. "A little smoke inhalation, some minor scratches and a few bruises are a small price to pay for what you went through last night."

"I know," I admit, as the tears start and I wipe them away, watching as the water trickles down my fingers, leaving a clean space on my filthy nails.

"You need to get more rest," she says, noticing my emotional state and I nod in agreement.

"Yes," says my dad agreeably, taking the hint. "We'll get going and let you sleep, love. We just wanted to be here when you woke up." He motions to Luke, who promptly hugs me and kisses me on the cheek.

"Look after yourself, sis," he says.

"We'll pop back in to see you later," says my dad, also bending to give me a hug. I pull him close and cling onto him tightly.

"Bye, Dad."

"Oh and I'll nip to your house this afternoon and bring you a few bits and pieces," adds Luke.

"Thanks," I whisper and attempt a smile. Once again, a sharp, stabbing pain shoots across my forehead, but I try to ignore it so that my dad and Luke don't notice. I give them a wave and watch silently as they leave the small ward; I then turn my attention back to the nurse.

"We want to keep you in for a couple of days, just to keep an eye on you," she says. I nod, already guessing as much.

"Decent guys those two," she remarks, as she hands me some tablets in a plastic container. "They've been here most of the night − worried sick about you."

"I know, they're the best," I admit, before reaching for the water and swallowing the tablets in one painful gulp.

Once I've taken the painkillers, the nurse leaves me alone to get more rest and, tucking myself back down under the sheets, I suddenly feel exhausted and lean back into the pillows to watch the world outside. Patients are starting to emerge for some early morning fresh air.

As I close my eyes once more, I quickly drift off to sleep and thank God for the stranger who saved my life, who I will probably never meet.

# Chapter 2

Will Travers lifted the chipped mug to his lips and took a sip of his second black coffee of the morning. Steam rose from the cup and stung his eyes, and he glanced at the clock on the kitchen wall, knowing full well that he had to get a move on. It was almost 8.30 a.m. and although he hadn't slept at all in almost 24 hours, he felt noticeably alert. The adrenaline from last night must still be pumping hard.

He wondered how Megan was doing. In fact, he hadn't stopped wondering since the moment he'd left her in the back of the ambulance last night, and he couldn't escape the feeling of guilt that plagued him for not getting to her sooner.

She had clung onto him for dear life and, as they'd raced back up to the deserted bridge, he could feel the desperation pouring from her. She was in shock and clearly distraught − hardly surprising after what she had been through. However, she was conscious when the ambulance arrived and the paramedics seemed optimistic that she would be fine.

He had fought all night with the demons in his head telling him that he should have gone to the hospital with her to make sure that she was OK, but he couldn't chance it. Not now.

Draining the last of his coffee, he put the empty mug in the sink, still full of dishes from the day before, and made his way upstairs. Entering his bedroom, he unwrapped the damp towel from around his waist and flung it onto the unmade bed, then bent to pull on a pair of jeans, which lay in a heap on the bedroom floor, from when he had returned late last night. There was still a faint smell of smoke from the fabric, and again thoughts of her filled his mind. Crossing the room, he opened the blinds, then halfheartedly picked out a fresh t-shirt from the wardrobe, pulling it over his pounding head. His ears were still blocked and ringing from the explosion. If he had been a few minutes later, Megan would be dead and maybe he would too.

Picking up his car keys and mobile from the kitchen table, he made his way out of his cottage and into the cool autumn air. Pausing on the doorstep, he held up a hand to shield his eyes and drew a deep breath. The low sun shone brightly and glistened against the water of the estuary, peeking through the gaps between the cottages lined in a row in front of his own. The temperature outside was colder today, much more so than yesterday. The hairs stood up on the surface of his skin and it forced him to stop and shudder. Rubbing his bare arms, he grabbed the cottage door before it closed behind him, and rushed back in to grab his jacket from the banister at the bottom of the stairs, where he always left it. However, today it wasn't there.

In that moment, Will realized how foolish he'd been! The jacket that he'd worn last night wasn't there, because he didn't come home with it.

"Shit!" he mouthed, his breath curling into a fog in the icy air as he stepped back outside and pulled his mobile from his back pocket. He had been so concerned about Megan that he hadn't retrieved the jacket he'd used as a blanket for her – she must still have it. Not that the jacket was of any real importance; yes, it was relatively expensive, and he had only bought it recently for comfort in the approaching harsh winter months, however, there was something in the pocket of that jacket that could potentially lead Megan directly to him, allowing her to discover his identity, question his reasons for being there and lead her straight to the truth!

# Chapter 3

Three days have gone by. I sit, perched eagerly on the end of my bed waiting for Luke to come and collect me from hospital, now keen to escape the confinement of the same four walls that I have been staring at since I woke up here. The small hospital ward is quiet today, with just me and an elderly lady in the bed opposite who was only admitted this morning, and is already snoring quietly. With her silver-grey hair flowing out across the white fabric of the pillow, and flawless creamy complexion, she looks peaceful and angelic. I can't help smiling to myself, and I wonder if my Mum would have been as beautiful had she made it to that age.

The medication that I've taken while in hospital has worked, and I now feel much better. The police came to see me yesterday and I told them everything I can remember – which isn't really that much. With the aches and pains alleviated, I'm now desperate to get back to my everyday life. I'm used to being on the go, and the slow pace and long, drawn-out hours here force me to relive the accident every day. I want to get back to work, focus my mind and try to forget about the accident; return to my habitual daily routine and the comfort of my own home.

I'm busy packing the items that my dad and Luke brought to hospital for me, when I see the jacket – it's at the bottom of the cabinet containing my belongings. I know immediately that it's not mine, and at first I think it's been left behind by the last patient to occupy the bed, but then I realize who it's likely to belong to. An image enters my head, as it has done almost every hour since the crash, of strong arms reaching into the car and pulling me to safety, and there's no doubt in my mind. *It's his jacket!*

Holding the padded fabric to my face, I inhale and breathe in a mixture of aftershave and smoke from the fire. A stab of pressure across my eyes triggers another flashback; his silhouette against the bright flames as we raced away from the burning car. I can still feel the heat radiating from his skin and hear the raspy desperation of his breathing, as he ran with me in his arms.

"Hi Megan!" I jump as my brother appears from nowhere and crouches down at eye level. "You almost ready to go?" he asks.

"Erm, yes, I think so." I smile and, lowering the jacket from Luke's view, I pull out the remainder of my belongings from the small cabinet, and quickly put the jacket in my holdall too.

"All ready to go," I reply.

Luke slings an arm loosely around my shoulders and propels me towards the exit of the ward.

"Let's get you home," he says, and I smile in agreement. That's the best thing I've heard during the 3 days I've been here.

***

I'm greeted at home by a living room full of fresh flowers, a pile of unopened 'get well soon' cards and my relieved-looking Ragdoll cat, Tilly. Although she loves Luke, who's been coming round to feed her during my absence, it's obvious that she's pleased I'm home and she wastes no time in jumping down from the sofa in the living room, wrapping herself around my legs and purring loudly. I bend down to stroke her and as Luke heads into the kitchen to put the kettle on, I turn to follow him, picking up a cloth before wiping down the granite worktops.

Luke takes the cloth angrily and flings it into the sink.

"For Christ's sake, Meg! Can you just forget about the cleaning for one day and focus on looking after yourself?!" He grabs me by the shoulders and turns me back in the direction of the lounge where he forces me onto the sofa next to Tilly.

"Now, sit down and relax!" he orders. On this rare occasion, I do as I'm told.

Luke makes sure I'm settled and then heads back to the kitchen to prepare me a cup of tea. My brother lives alone and, as a single and carefree bachelor, he is as far removed from a domestic god as you can get, but he does make the best cup of tea I've ever tasted. It feels strange and a little disturbing that he is the one caring for me today. Since our mum died, it's always been the other way around; I've looked after both Luke and Dad for the past 11 years. I'm used to being the one in charge and, as a self-proclaimed control freak, I am already finding this situation a little difficult to accept.

Luke comes back into the lounge and hands me a steaming mug of tea. I accept it and cradle it in my already clammy hands.

"It's so nice to be home," I admit, taking a look around the slightly disorganized room. Already, I'm mentally planning what needs to be done as soon as Luke leaves.

"Don't you start rushing around, Meg. The doctor says you need to rest and I think for once in your life you should listen to someone who knows what they're talking about."

"Yes, don't worry, I will." I answer, already knowing what will happen the moment my brother sets foot out of the door.

\*\*\*

Luke stays with me for a little while, then makes a move to go after confirming that him and Dad will come and see me tomorrow. Things have been far from easy in my life lately and I am grateful that I have two such loving men as part of it.

I settle back down onto the sofa next to Tilly and begin to open the cards. Most are from family members and work colleagues wishing me well and hoping I'm better soon. Their kind words and loving messages make me feel a fraud in some ways, because, apart from a little pain in my left knee from banging the steering column, and the cut above my eye that looks far worse than it really is, I do feel much better. I can't remember the last time I was absent from work because, apart from bereavement leave, I've dragged myself into the office every day since I started at the company 8 years ago.

I prop the cards along the mantelpiece before rearranging the vases of flowers on the window sill, and I begin to tidy up. I'd actually forgotten about the jacket in my bag and, as I'm emptying the contents into the washing machine, I catch sight of it again.

Pulling it out, I unfold it, hold it out in front of me and study it, as the familiar aroma of aftershave and smoke rises up from it again.

The jacket is a black, waterproof design with a heavy fur-trimmed hood. The label tells me that it's men's size 'large' and, if I know my designer brands correctly, I can guess it has a hefty price tag. I instantly feel guilty. The man who saved me obviously put it over me and forgot to take it with him. I search the pockets for some form of ID in the hope that I can trace him and return it, or maybe buy him a new one, but I find nothing. I'm beginning to fold it up again when I notice that there's a concealed inside pocket that I haven't checked - I reach inside and pull out a key.

The key looks like the type you get in a hotel, with a large rectangular shaped keyring attached, and on turning it over I see that it holds an address for a property based in Morteford – somewhere I've never visited before, but have heard is very charming.

I place the coat neatly on the kitchen bench before returning to my chores. Maybe I'll give it a few days and pay the stranger a visit; it's the least I can do. He saved me and I owe him my life.

# Chapter 4

Charlotte Taylor pulled back the heavy duvet and eased herself from her bed. The polished wooden floor was cold and unsatisfying against her warm feet – almost as 'chilly' as her blind date last night! Yet she'd still woken up, in her underwear, next to the guy, with a pounding headache and an intense feeling of self-loathing. Smirnoff and loneliness is never a good combination, and by now she should have learnt that lesson. Charlotte had always vowed that she would never go on a blind date and, this morning, she realized why.

Creeping across the room in search of her clothes, she risked a quick peek behind her at the man her mother had insisted she meet up with last night. The son of her mother's friend, Margaret, from her book club, was lying sprawled out on top of the sheets, sleeping soundly and wearing nothing but a smile! Although pretty good-looking, with a hell of a body and semi-decent bedroom skills, he had also clearly undertaken a sense-of-humour bypass and his personality was as dead as a corpse (and she had seen a lot of corpses in her time!).

As Charlotte retrieved her clothes, which had been thrown to various locations in her date's large loft-style bedroom, she racked her brain. For the life of her, she couldn't remember his name; Daniel, Damien, Dominic…? She was certain it began with a 'D'. Either way, it was another confirmation that her mum doesn't 'always know best', and that she certainly doesn't know her daughter nearly as well as she would like to believe.

Navigating her way to the kitchen at the bottom of a spiral-shaped iron staircase, Charlotte tore her stare away from the outlandishly modern-looking appliances and showy gadgets that dotted the room. She began rummaging through the drawers in search of painkillers to try and dull the now fully blown headache and, finally, she found some paracetamol, quickly swallowing two capsules with the remnants of a half-finished, lipstick-stained glass of Moet.

She tried to remember the chain of events when they got back last night, playing them in sequence through her mind, like scenes from a half-baked saucy film, but the vodka and champagne had achieved their job of wiping clean the better part of her memory. She could remember the taxi ride back, and a quick fumble on the sofa, but after that, it all became slightly blurry.

Searching the living room for her phone, Charlotte grabbed the coordinating scatter cushions from the expensive looking leather sofa, and quickly found it tucked down the side of the seat, along with her date's discarded boxers.

Taking a quick look at the screen before putting the phone into her bag, she registered the five unread texts sent from her mother last night, all no doubt asking how things were going with Darren, *Darren that was it!* She dreaded speaking to her later, she never liked letting her mum down and she knew she secretly held high hopes that Charlotte and Darren would hit it off. Chances were she'd already been out wedding outfit shopping.

Charlotte rushed to the apartment door as soon as she heard a creak from the floorboards above, cowardly deciding to make a dash for it while she could. She had never been one for awkward moments, and chose to give this one a rapid swerve.

She managed to get out of the apartment block and onto the street below without anyone seeing her, and luckily, without Mr Boring stirring any further. With the building now behind her, the walk of shame successfully executed, and the hangover already starting to ease with the fresh air, she felt quite smug and was deliberating a sausage McMuffin or full English when her phone started to ring. She sighed loudly before reaching into her silver clutch bag to answer it, half expecting it to be her mother.

"Oh, hi Tony! How can I help you on this beautiful autumn day?" she asked, cheerily.

"Christ, Charlotte, you sound rather chirpy for this time on a Sunday morning," responded Tony, in an unenthusiastic tone.

"Yeah, well. What can I say?"

"The blind date went well last night then?" asked Tony, as facetious as ever.

"Nope, the date was abysmal, but I've got the day off and a McDonalds 12 feet away from me, so things could be worse!"

Tony laughed, "well, unfortunately you might have to make that breakfast a takeaway."

Charlotte quickly registered the information that Tony relayed and prepared to wave goodbye to the Sunday she had planned; heading back to her flat after breakfast, lazing in front of the TV, indulging in her own weight in chocolate, and forgetting all about her responsibilities. That was until the next morning, when she would wake to the 6.20 alarm and dive back into her job with the passion and determination that she'd had every day since becoming a Detective Inspector.

Charlotte started to pace back and forth in an attempt to stay warm. She hadn't worn a coat last night and hadn't really noticed the cold, but she could definitely do with one now.

"Please tell me you're joking Tony. They really need us to work – today?"

"Sorry, something's come up and we need to go on a little road trip."

"A road trip? But we haven't had a full day off in weeks. Anyway, aren't you supposed to be on holiday for a couple of days?" Charlotte couldn't hide the disappointment in her voice.

"That's cancelled! All part and parcel of our job, I'm afraid sweetheart," replied Tony. "Besides, I'm no good without my partner in crime now am I?"

"What's happened?" asked Charlotte. She stopped pacing as a group of teenage boys walked past her and scurried into the restaurant. The last of the pack, a boy of around 14 with straggly, greasy hair and a face full of acne, stopped to noticeably check out her breasts, his eyes nearly popping out of their sockets, before entering the restaurant behind the rest of the group. She glanced down at her blouse and realized that, in her rush to get away this morning, she'd not fastened it correctly and her black lace bra was visible for all to see.

"Shit!" She tucked her phone under her chin and, before turning away from the restaurant windows, she proceeded to redo the buttons. The strong smell of her blind date's heavy aftershave clung to her skin and her stomach churned.

"We need to get up to Newcastle ASAP," said Tony. His voice was now deadly serious, as was Charlotte's, when she replied.

"Why, what's in Newcastle?" Charlotte was already moving away from McDonalds, her eyes searching the Sunday morning traffic for the nearest taxi. She had a feeling she knew what Tony was going to tell her.

"Rick Donovan," answered Tony, instantly confirming her suspicions. "It looks like he's back!"

# Chapter 5

Will pushed through the aging wooden doors of the Anchor pub and confidently wound his way through the crowd. It was late Sunday afternoon and, as always during the weekend, the place was crammed. Hardly surprising though as the village of Morteford only had three pubs and this was the only one that served a half-decent pint.

The Anchor Tavern was what the typical Brit would affectionately refer to as a 'real pub'. Living up to its name as being one of Morteford's oldest listed buildings, it had retained most of its original features. There were no swanky furnishings, innovative gastro food, or ludicrously priced cocktails in sight; just a few dated wooden tables and chairs, yellowing floral wallpaper clashing with red-patterned carpets, and the occasional homemade steak and ale pie, together with a huge open fire to welcome you on a cold autumn afternoon.

Will shrugged off his coat and threw it onto the rickety old stand in the corner, then paused to rub his hands in front of the fire before heading to the bar.

"Alright, Will?" Mike, the Anchor's owner, greeted Will from behind the bar and bypassed a few rare non-locals to make his way over to him.

"Same as normal, young sir?" Mike reached for a pint glass beneath him.

"Yeah, cheers Mike." Will stuck his hand into the pocket of his jeans to pull out his wallet. "Is Elliott in yet?"

Mike scanned the busy pub and returned his attention to Will.

"Can't say I've seen him."

Will nodded as Mike began pulling a pint of Carling.

"How's your dad doing mate?" Genuine concern filled Mike's voice.

As a regular in the Anchor, and a Morteford resident for over 40 years, Will's dad was sorely missed. His absence around the village these past few months hadn't gone unnoticed, and even though the extent of his father's illness had been played down by both Will and his mother, his father's daily non-attendance for a quick teatime pint spoke volumes.

"He's as well as can be expected," replied Will, before accepting the pint and taking a well-needed sip.

"And your mum?"

"Yeah, she's not bad, holding it together pretty well really."

"Good, well send your dad my regards the next time you visit him will you, and tell your mum I was asking after her."

"Will do, thanks Mike," smiled Will, sliding money across the bar before making his way to the far end of the pub.

He chose to sit in his and Elliott's usual spot – next to the window and the open fire – looking out over the estuary with a clear view of the small town of Fadstow, a short boat trip across the water. Of course the seats were empty when he made his way over. The Anchor was the sort of place where each seat had an invisible name tag and, over the weekend, it was a known fact that these two belonged to Will and Elliott.

Will sat down and sighed loudly, then stretched his long legs out under the table in front of him. His joints screamed out in protest and he ached from head to toe. Carrying Megan away from the wreckage on Thursday night had made him realize how unfit he had become. Years of manual labour in the local shipyard had kept him on top of his fitness, but the two and a half years of running his father's old business, based primarily behind an office desk, were now noticeably beginning to take their toll on his once enviable physique.

Picking up his pint he took a well-deserved gulp and spun round in his seat to look out of the window in an attempt to stop his racing thoughts.

Although he had lived here for all of his 35 years, Will never tired of that view. Even on a chilly autumn afternoon like this, the vast waters of the estuary, maze of winding cobbled alleys, and brightly painted fishermen's cottages that lined the streets of his home village never failed to tug at his heartstrings.

Usually, this is the place he would come to unwind with Elliott after they'd endured a stressful week at work together, or to sit and enjoy a quiet pint alone, contemplating after a visit to the care home to see his dad. Usually the view alone would succeed in calming him. Tonight though, it simply didn't come near.

No more than 10 minutes had passed before Elliott pulled up his chair opposite Will and placed his bottle of cider next to his. Will was relieved; the past 10 minutes had been filled with acquaintances passing his table and asking how he was holding up; wanting to talk to him about his father's rapidly worsening health. Morteford was a diminutive village and everyone knew about his dad's current battle against cancer. It was evident that people were concerned and, although he was grateful for their kindness, he was simply not in the mood for polite conversation tonight.

"You alright, mate?" asked Elliott.

Will studied the face of his oldest friend and, as he settled down opposite him, he noticed his worried look. Just like Will, Elliott was an only child, and the two men were like brothers. Will could turn to Elliott for anything, and he hoped that the feeling was mutual. He was the only one who knew the full story – about Megan and where Will had been 3 nights ago; what had happened. He'd called Elliott to fill him in, the morning after he had returned to Morteford, and he had been totally shocked!

"I've been better mate," replied Will honestly, rubbing at his rarely unshaven chin.

"You look like hell!"

"Cheers."

"Do you know how she's doing?" asked Elliott.

Will looked down at the battered wooden table and picked at the corner of the peeling beermat that his drink was resting on, the feeling of guilt once again surging through him like an electrical current.

"No, but I'm sure she'll be fine," he answered sheepishly, finally looking back at Elliott.

Elliott took a gulp of cider and nodded thoughtfully, before rolling up the sleeves of his chunky knitted jumper and placing his hands on his knees.

"So, where do you go from here?"

Will sighed and shrugged his shoulders before draining what was left in his glass and placing it back on the table.

"I really don't know, but I've got a favour to ask of you El, a *really* big favour."

Elliott leaned back in his seat, smiled warmly, and replied in a way that Will had been hoping for.

"Just name it, mate."

# Chapter 6

I'm on the phone to my friend Eva, when a black Vauxhall Insignia pulls up outside my living-room window, and a man and woman climb out, making their way to my front door.

"Eva, I'll have to call you back. There's somebody coming to the door," I follow their shadows, cast by the early morning light, up the driveway, until I can no longer see them.

"Yes, no problem, Meg, I've got to get off to work anyway – I really just wanted to check that you got home from hospital OK?" replies Eva.

"I did, and I'm fine, honestly. Thanks for calling Eva."

"Alright, Meg, look after yourself!"

I finish the call, set my mug down and, as the bell goes for the second time, I hurry to the door, wondering who my surprise visitors are at such an early hour on a Monday morning.

"Hi, can I help?" I ask, as the couple I've never seen before, smile pleasantly. The man takes a step closer; he looks to be in his early forties, the woman maybe a little younger. I can tell their profession before they even introduce themselves.

"Hi Mrs Cooper. I'm Detective Chief Inspector Morgan, and this is Detective Inspector Taylor." The man flashes a warrant card before my eyes. "Do you have a few moments to spare – we would like a quick chat with you, if that's alright?" He takes another step forward.

"Yes, of course," I reply, stepping to one side to allow the smartly dressed detectives into my home. Confusion sets in as I take them through to the living room and gesture for them to sit down. I offer to make them a coffee before we talk, unsure about the etiquette for a police visit. Both detectives politely decline.

"Nice place," says DCI Morgan. He takes a brief look around the room as he settles into the sofa nearest to the window, turning to glance at the view behind him. The hills of the Northumberland countryside are shrouded in early morning fog, the grey clouds above outlined by the haze of imperceptible rays.

"Lovely area too, my wife's brother lives close by and I used to live not too far from here myself," he adds, turning his focus back to me.

"Really?" I smile, trying to show interest, but honestly, I couldn't care less. I want to know their reasons for being here.

"Can I ask what this is about?" I ask, balancing myself on the edge of the opposite sofa and crossing my ankles uncomfortably.

"We're sorry to barge in on you first thing on a Monday," says DI Taylor. She unbuttons her navy mac and removes her brightly coloured scarf before sitting down next to Morgan on the sofa. Her accent isn't local, instead revealing a clear Cockney twang. "We realize you were only discharged from hospital yesterday afternoon following the car accident," she adds.

I nod, feeling even more confused.

"We won't take up much of your time, we promise," says Morgan, reassuringly.

"Is this about the crash then?" I ask impatiently, focusing my attention on DCI Morgan. He places his hands on his knees and leans forward, his grey suit jacket pulling tightly across his torso.

"Yes, as I said, we just have a few questions Mrs Cooper," he responds, in a clear Geordie dialect and as he leans further forward, his broad shoulders block the minimal amount of daylight coming through the small nearby window. His intimidating presence makes me nervous.

"Please, just call me Megan," I say. The words come out rather frostier than I had intended; my married name is a firm reminder of the pain I endured last year and at times it's too hard to hear. This is one of those times.

"OK Megan. Could you explain what happened on Thursday night please, and how you ended up steering off Kitley Bridge?"

"I've already told the police about this," I reply, feeling irritated. "Two officers came to visit me yesterday morning while I was still in hospital and they took a statement from me then."

"Yes, you spoke to Sergeant Thompson and PC McLean, but if you can just tell us what you told them?" says DI Taylor. She smiles, and her perfectly made-up face and bouncy blonde hair makes me feel unattractive in comparison. I instinctively touch my own hair, smoothing it over the shoulders of my sweatshirt, before I clear my still-sore throat to continue.

"I was driving home from work on Thursday night…" My voice instantly breaks. I hold up my hand and cough before I start to reiterate the exact story I had told the police officers in hospital.

"You work as a marketing manager at Brightdale House in Newcastle city centre, is that correct?" interrupts Morgan, before I barely begin.

I nod. "Yes, I'd been holding a late meeting, so didn't finish work till after 7 pm, and it's a 40-minute drive home. I was only 10 minutes from home when the crash happened."

DI Taylor jots down a few notes on a pad and then focuses her attention on me, silently coaxing me to continue the account.

"There's not a lot to tell," I admit. "There was a car coming towards me; it didn't slow down, and when I tried to brake it didn't work."

"And the car approaching you definitely didn't attempt to reduce its speed?" asks Morgan.

"No."

"How fast would you say the other car was going?"

"It must have been travelling at least 60 miles per hour when I hit the bridge, that's why I had to try and steer to avoid it. I lost control of my car and came off the road." I shudder as I am suddenly back in the car, flying through the air, branches scratching the windows and pounding on the roof, glass shattering in front of me.

"Did you get a good look at the other car?" asks Morgan.

"Not really."

"You told Sergeant Thompson that you believed the other car to be a white SUV?"

"Yes, I think so."

Morgan nods, "and did you say that you were having problems with your brakes before the accident?"

"Yes," my gaze falls to the floor. "I'd been meaning to get them looked at, but just haven't had the time." I think of Luke, hounding me to get the car checked when the brakes started sticking a couple of weeks back, and now feeling a complete fool for not listening to him.

"You told the police that a man pulled you from the car, approximately 10 minutes after you went off the side of the bridge, Megan?" asks Taylor.

"I think it was only around 10 minutes, but it could have been a lot longer. I'm not too sure of the exact timeframe, to be honest."

"That's OK," replies Morgan. "You also said that you were carried back up to the road leading to the bridge?"

"Yes. We staggered together from the car and then he covered me with a jacket and carried me the rest of the way."

"The gentleman carried you back to the road leading to the bridge?" Taylor confirms.

"Yes."

"And you don't know who this man is?"

"No."

"Can you remember anything at all about him?"

"No – I didn't get a good enough look. It was really dark, I was in shock and too much of a state to be fully aware of what was going on."

"That's understandable, given the circumstances." Morgan flashes me a gentle smile.

"The only thing I can remember is that he had black boots on, and a very strong aftershave." I offer, feeling wholly useless. "Also, I think he burnt his hand when he tried to open the car door. I noticed it was injured when he reached over to unclip my seatbelt."

"So then he lifted you up to the road and called for an ambulance?" asks Taylor.

"I think so, but it's all still very hazy."

"He didn't accompany you to the hospital?"

"No, my brother spoke to the paramedics who looked after me that night. The man called for an ambulance and waited for it to arrive, but they had to rush me straight off and he didn't give his name." I recite word for word what Luke had told me on the Friday morning in hospital.

Taylor and Morgan glance at each other.

"You said the man covered you with a jacket?" asks Morgan.

"Yes."

"Do you still have that jacket Megan, or did he retrieve it before you got into the ambulance?" asks Morgan, adding "any evidence at this point is greatly appreciated."

I move to retrieve the jacket from the kitchen bench where I left it. *Evidence? Why the hell are they collecting evidence? The man saved me!*

Removing the key and concealing it in the pocket of my sweatshirt, I return to the lounge and hand the jacket to Taylor. She carefully studies the front of it.

"What about the blood?" she asks, noticing a small red stain on the left shoulder, which before now I hadn't spotted.

"I think that must be mine." I touch my head, trailing my finger along the line of small stitches running parallel with my eyebrow, and then adjusting my fringe to cover them again.

Taylor slides the jacket into a large clear bag, which leads me to question the real reasons they are here.

"Can I ask why you are involved?" I ask, as politely as possible. "Like I say, the local police have already been through all this. They think the car was probably stolen by kids, so just a typical case of Thursday night joyriding in a small country town where there's very little else for them to do. It's a frighteningly common thing."

Morgan seems to ignore this statement.

"Have you ever heard of a man named Rick Donovan?" asks Morgan. His question is a little random and catches me off guard.

"No," I answer immediately. I don't even need time to think – I'm good at remembering names, and a skill I've always prided myself on. Years of being a manager with a large team and a high turnover of staff has given me the ability to remember names incredibly well, and I know straight away that this name has absolutely no meaning to me.

"OK, well, I think that's all we need for now," replies Morgan abruptly, suddenly standing and straightening his jacket. Taylor wraps her scarf back around her neck before following Morgan out into the hall.

"Thank you for your time, Mrs Cooper." The two detectives return to the front door and I see them out. As I close the door behind them and hear their car pull away from my drive, I wonder what they are investigating and who the hell Rick Donovan is.

# Chapter 7

Tony couldn't help but reminisce as he and Charlotte made their way along the Northumberland coastal route after leaving Megan Cooper's house. Feeling nostalgic, he'd purposely chosen a detour so that he could drive part of the route, knowing that Charlotte would be none the wiser to his cunning plan.

Tony liked where he lived now. He'd become fond of his life in the North West and he loved the fact that his family was so happy and settled there. However, Tony's heart would always be in the North East, and every time he came back to visit, it only reaffirmed the fact. He would always be a Geordie lad at heart!

Glancing across at Charlotte, who was in her own world staring out of the window, he pulled onto the A19 and checked the car's illuminated clock. Even though it was now approaching 9 am, the sky above remained gloomy over the surrounding farmer's fields and a dense grey fog floated on the horizon, fast approaching from the nearby North Sea. He switched on the car's headlights and cancelled the unnecessary sat nav instructions, telling him where he should be going. He had driven this road hundreds of times and knew each part of it like the back of his hand, so could probably drive it blindfolded if he had to.

Charlotte reached forward and changed the radio station. Tony was impressed! In the first half an hour of her being picked up yesterday, not only had she already programmed in all of her favourite stations, and figured out how to operate the stupidly complicated sat nav, but she had also successfully paired his mobile to the car's system and worked out the hands free. These were actions that Tony hadn't fathomed in the whole time he'd been driving the car.

Charlotte had been uncharacteristically quiet since they'd left Megan's home, and he knew that it would be less than 5 minutes before her thoughts would eventually spill out. It took 2!

"That house she has is something pretty special, hey?" she asked, her attention still fixed on the road ahead.

"Yes, not that big, but *very* nice. Fabulous location, and I bet the views from the back garden, over the countryside, are stunning."

"I agree it has nice views, but I reckon it would be a bit dull living out in the sticks like that. Anyway, sheep are highly overrated, Tony."

"Jealous much, Taylor?"

Charlotte ignored Tony and continued with her trail of thought that Tony was yet to guess.

"You said Olivia's brother lives in the same area as Megan Cooper?"

"Close yeah, why?"

"How much do you think a house like that goes for?"

"Well, Ewan bought his house 5 years ago, and didn't get much change from a million." Tony thought about his brother-in-law. Although a decent enough bloke, he never missed an opportunity to gloat about his wealth, and he was full of his own self-importance. Tony always thought narcissism an ugly trait to possess.

"Christ, what does her brother do to be able to afford a place like that?"

"Plastic surgeon."

"Ha," Charlotte raised her eyebrows, "I always knew I was in the wrong profession."

"Don't kid yourself, Charlotte, it's obvious that you love what you do."

Charlotte paused to consider, before replying, "Yeah, but I'd also *really* like a fancy crystal chandelier, like the one in Megan's hallway."

"I'll bear that in mind as a wedding gift, for when you eventually get married."

"You'll be waiting a while then!"

Tony laughed. "Nah, I wouldn't be so sure."

"And who do you think I'm going to marry? I can't hold down a relationship for longer than 4 months!"

"Our Shaun has taken a bit of a fancy to you, you know. Hasn't stopped asking about you since the summer, when you showed up at Liv's 40th barbecue."

Charlotte laughed – Tony's younger brother was a great guy, with the same family values and hardworking ethic as his older brother. Coupled with a similar build and handsome features, there was no denying that Shaun Morgan was a catch, but the thought of going out with her boss's brother just didn't sit right.

"I'm happy on my own for the time being, but thanks for the advice, Cupid!"

"Nobody's happy on their own! It's just something single people tell themselves to feel better," Tony joked.

Charlotte sat forward in her seat, suddenly registering the road signs for the coast.

"Tony, where are we going? I thought we had to get back to headquarters?"

"We do, but we're just popping in to see my mam first."

Charlotte chuckled, "Just because we're working in your neck of the woods doesn't entitle you to a whistle-stop tour of the Morgan family! And I'm not sure Emery would be overly impressed if he knew."

"Don't be daft! Anyway, it was his idea. Mam is expecting us and she said she'll have the coffee and bacon butties ready for when we get there."

"OK, you've twisted my arm." Charlotte shook her head before changing the topic of conversation back to work and away from her car-crash excuse of a love life, and bacon sandwiches.

"The car Megan was driving when she crashed was a pretty decent one as well. I saw the reports that Emery gave you."

"Aye, it was brand new," agreed Tony. "Seems strange that the brakes were dodgy after the short mileage she had done in it."

"So, she could afford a car that cost more or less £20,000, but couldn't fork out for a mechanic to check the brakes?"

"That's not what she was saying – she just hadn't had the time to get them looked at. Anyway, I really don't think it *was* an underlying problem."

"What do you mean?"

"I'm not convinced it was a coincidence that her brakes failed on that night."

"So you don't think her brakes were faulty at all?"

"Possibly."

"You mean, you think someone tampered with her brakes before the accident?"

"The investigators who went down to the crash site don't seem to think so, and even if the brakes had been tampered with before the accident, there's no way of knowing now. The explosion destroyed the small amount that was left of the car after the fire."

"What did you say she did for work?" asked Charlotte.

"She's a marketing manager for a big retail chain."

"And she can afford to keep a house like that on her salary, and have leftover cash for a little sporty number?"

"You don't know people's circumstances, Charlotte."

Tony didn't feel the need to discuss the financial details right now. Although he hadn't pried too much into Megan Cooper's background, he had access to it, and he guessed from the small amount that he had seen that her deceased husband had left her financially secure, via his will and life insurance.

Charlotte ignored Tony's comment and continued to dig.

"What did her husband do?"

"He was some sort of account manager for a building firm based over in Gateshead."

Tony had only read details about Megan Cooper when he and Charlotte had arrived in Newcastle yesterday afternoon, and, after catching up with his old boss in Northumbria CID, and speaking with the officers who'd already questioned Megan, he had headed to his hotel armed with information. He had then spent a few hours reading the notes and had been awake into the small hours of this morning running things through his head.

It seemed to him that Megan Cooper had been dealt a fairly shitty hand so far, and she was only 30. Her mother had died when she was in her late teens, and then her partner of 9 years, with whom she had been married to for 5, had been cruelly taken from her too. Tony knew that even Charlotte wasn't shallow enough to believe that the money made up for this loss, and the sadness in her expression at the mere mention of her late husband's name had said at all.

Tony hoped that this was all just an unfortunate coincidence. His ex-boss, Joe Emery, had called him yesterday morning and said that the local authorities believed that Rick Donovan had nothing to do with Megan Cooper's accident, and that the crash was just another pothole in her long road of bad luck. Tony had been in the game for long enough now to know that indeed, coincidences did happen, however, the word 'coincidence' and Rick Donovan had rarely been strung together in the same sentence.

Tony called Emery to update him and to confirm that everything Megan had told them this morning had coincided with her earlier statement while in hospital. Emery thanked him for his time today and promised to keep him updated if any more information arose.

As they continued along the road towards his parents' home in Whitley Bay, Tony crossed his fingers and prayed that the local police were correct, and that this time, for once, he had it all totally wrong.

# Chapter 8

It's been 2 days since the visit from the uninvited detectives. They haven't been in touch with me again and I'm assuming that, whatever information I provided has given them the answers they need, and quashed any link with Rick Donovan.

It's Wednesday night, and after a boring few days of sitting around the house, because my boss insisted I take the full week off, I'm eager to get out and spend some time away from home. Although the rest and relaxation has made me feel a lot better, the time off has also meant a lot of hours on my own and, with an unoccupied mind, I have exhausted my own company!

Eva and I have arranged to meet outside a bar and, when I arrive, she's already waiting.

"Hi Eva, sorry I'm a bit late, the taxi wasn't on time," I say, greeting my friend with a peck on the cheek. As always, she looks impeccable and I expect nothing less from my closest friend.

"No problem," replies Eva, dancing on the spot to stay warm. "I've been chatted up three times already – standing here does wonders for a girl's ego!" She smiles brightly.

"Come on, let's get hammered," I say, linking her arm and heading for the open door.

The popular wine bar is busy. Fake cobwebs dress the walls, and large plastic spiders hang from the ceiling. Small pumpkins with lit candles sit on each table, and the bar area is surrounded by people donning an array of imaginative fancy dress costumes.

'Halloween' to me is for children and, as I don't have any, and I don't agree with the money-making, over-the-top event that it's become, I tend to avoid it. However, looking around tonight, it's clear to see there are plenty of people who do like to get involved!

Pushing my way through the crowd, I accept that we're not going to achieve the quiet weekday drink that we had hoped for; nevertheless I head straight to the bar. It only takes a few minutes before I'm greeted by the barmaid, aka Frankenstein's wife. I order our drinks while Eva stands behind me, being propositioned by a questionable-looking Dracula.

We're lucky to find an empty booth at the back of the pub, where it's a little quieter to sit and chat. I've only spoken to Eva a couple of times since the accident, but she knows all about the detectives' visit earlier in the week.

"So, how are you *really* feeling?" asks Eva, as she sits down, places a bottle of Prosecco in front of us and fills our glasses.

"Yeah, I'm fine thanks – just itching to get back to work if I'm honest."

"You never were the type to take it easy," she replies, taking a sip from her glass. "Are you still thinking about finding the guy who saved you?"

"I'm not sure now. I gave his jacket to the police on Monday, so I have no real need."

"Aren't you curious about him though?"

"Well, yeah, I suppose." I take a sip of Prosecco and the bubbles tingle my tongue; the alcohol that I have recently abstained from tastes wonderful after the stressful time I have had.

"Well, why don't you go? You have the address printed on that key, don't you?"

"Yes, it's on the keyring it was attached to."

"So…what you waiting for?" Eva refills our glasses; the alcohol hasn't touched the sides.

"I'll tell you what," adds Eva, "I'll come with you. We'll make a little break of it this weekend and, as you don't have a car yet, I'll drive! It'll do us both some good.

I still shudder at the thought of being behind the wheel of a car so soon after the accident; it makes me feel sick.

"Do you even know how to get there?"

"That's what sat navs are for Meg!"

"Have you been to Morteford before though?" I ask.

"Of course! Lots of times actually - mum and dad used to take Johnny and I every summer when we were kids."

My heart races at the mention of her twin brother's name, prompting me to glance at the wedding ring on my left hand. I roll it between my thumb and forefinger thoughtfully; our initials and wedding date fastidiously engraved on the inside.

"I'd forgotten – he'd told me that," I whisper.

Eva reaches across the table and gently rubs my hand.

"I miss him too, Meg," she says, tears fill her heavily made-up eyes briefly before she brushes them away and picks up her glass.

"Let's raise a toast to him," she says, enthusiastically. I smile and hold up my glass against hers.

"To Johnny!" she declares loudly. "The best brother and husband a girl could ever wish for – gone but never forgotten."

I manage a smile through my tears.

"To Johnny."

\*\*\*

A taxi eventually brings me home and I feel more relaxed than I have these past few days; it's definitely done me some good.

Slipping off my heels in the hallway, I flex my throbbing toes and head to the kitchen to pour myself a glass of water. The house is so quiet you could hear a pin drop.

I'm used to that now, but at first, after Johnny died, I couldn't bear the silence. Even though, towards the end, I spent a lot of time on my own in the house, I knew that no matter how late it was, he would be home. When I first lost him, it took a long time before I accepted that he wasn't coming back. I would sleep with the light on and, although I wasn't keen on the darkness, it was the quiet of the house that really unsettled me.

Downing a half pint of water in an attempt to wake up hangover-free in the morning, I head upstairs where I change into a pair of comfortable cotton pyjamas and climb wearily into bed. Tilly follows me and curls into a furry ball at the left side of the duvet – Johnny's side – and, since he died, there hasn't been a single night when she hasn't fallen asleep in the exact same spot. I'm asleep before my head hits the pillow.

Half an hour later, I'm wakened by a loud shattering sound downstairs. Startled, I look around the dark bedroom, trying to get my bearings, with my brain swirling in a concoction of sleep-filled fog and alcohol-induced disorientation. My eyes settle on Tilly, still curled in a ball fast asleep at the bottom of the bed, and suddenly my heart starts pounding as realization washes over me. *If it wasn't the cat making that noise, then what was it?*

Throwing back the heavy duvet, I lower myself to the carpet and creep to the door. Moving to the landing, I stop at the top of the stairs and flick on the light switch, before tiptoeing down. I quickly cross the hall, the cold marble stinging my warm feet, and it's then that I hear the sound of running water coming from the kitchen.

I run the short distance from the hallway and through the open door of the kitchen. I don't click on the light, but I can clearly see what woke me – the kitchen tap is running full blast, and the sink, now full of water due to the plug being in, is overflowing down the sides of the cupboards. The glass, which had been in the empty sink, now lies shattered on the tiles and the floor is gleaming with large puddles deepening by the second; the patio door is also slightly ajar.

"Shit!" I shout into the freezing cold, empty room. How could I have been so stupid? I must have left the tap running when I got a drink before bed, however, I don't know how the plug's in, enabling it to flood! I must have done that without realizing – aswell as leaving the patio door open when I let Tilly in before going to bed. *I'm never drinking again!*

I quickly turn off the heavy flow of cold water and, after I discard the broken glass, I race back upstairs to get some towels. My heart's still leaping in my chest at the shock of being woken so suddenly.

I reach the kitchen again, pausing in the doorway as light from the hall illuminates the water still pooling on the shiny floor. I take a deep breath and try my best to ignore the vision of Johnny I see in my head – he's standing in the centre of the pool, dripping wet. His body is still, his skin pale and his once bright blue eyes are lifeless as he watches me.

"Just ignore it Meg, it's not real," I say aloud to the empty kitchen, bending to put the armful of towels down on the floor to soak up the mess at his bare feet.

Once the majority of the water is cleaned up, I throw the sodden towels into the washing machine, setting the timer to start first thing in the morning. I then wearily head back upstairs. Climbing into the now cold bed, where Tilly hasn't even stirred during the commotion, I pull the duvet up to my chin, a sudden chill entering the hot, centrally heated room.

I roll onto my right side and close my eyes. As I do most nights, I imagine Johnny climbing into bed behind me, and pulling me towards him, like he used to in the early days. I imagine his warm breath against my neck as he tells me that he loves me and, as I drift off to sleep, I imagine the gentle rhythm of his heartbeat that is no longer there.

# Chapter 9

Charlotte raised the burger to her lips and took an unladylike mouthful.

"God, I've been waiting for this since Sunday," she murmured. Tony, who was sitting opposite in the service station fast-food restaurant nursing a large cappuccino, smirked at her.

"How do you eat so much and manage to stay so thin?" he asked, as she finished the burger and wiped away the mustard that dotted the corners of her mouth.

It was true that since Tony had hit 40, the middle-age spread had taken hold, and even though he looked after himself and was in relatively good shape, he still couldn't achieve the desired results without working hard at it. Charlotte, on the other hand, was only a few years younger than Tony, but her tiny figure, washboard stomach and toned limbs were a scientific marvel. She'd never set foot in a gym in her life, and lived on a diet that consisted of fast food and takeaways.

"I do lots of physical activity!" she answered, still with her mouth full and reaching for the extra-large Coke in front of her.

"Yeah, we know about your type of physical activity," joked Tony.

"You're just jealous Tony, admit it." Charlotte smiled and playfully hit her colleague on the arm.

"I'm a happily married man DI Taylor, and I have an *extremely* sexy wife back at home," he retorted, dead pan and adopting the stern professional voice he always used when questioning suspects.

Charlotte laughed. "I know, I know, I'm only joking."

Tony Morgan was the best DCI Charlotte had ever had the pleasure to work alongside and she knew his sense of humour matched hers – the main reason they'd become such good friends, as well as colleagues, over the 2 years they had worked together. She also knew his limits, and how far she could push him. After Charlotte had transferred from the London Met, and Tony had relocated to Manchester with his family, they had both found themselves in the same boat; new city, new team and both ultimately thrown in at the deep end of their respective new roles. Charlotte had a tremendous amount of respect for Tony – she had learned a lot from him and, although they had a laid-back relationship, she was always aware of him being her superior.

"How is Olivia?" she asked Tony.

"She's fine. A bit pissed off that we have to go back to Newcastle, but she understands that needs must. She said 'hi', by the way."

Charlotte smiled, "…and the kids?"

"They're good. Isla lost another tooth last night; she'll have none left if she keeps going at this rate."

"There'll be a visit from the tooth fairy to your house soon then?"

"Yep, and Liv's giving her £5 a pop! I swear Isla is yanking them out herself now just to pocket the cash." Tony replied.

Charlotte grinned, "Smart kid! How's Archie?"

"He's fine, although almost knocked himself out at nursery yesterday pretending to be Spiderman. Liv was in A&E for almost 2 hours waiting to get him checked over."

"But he's OK?"

"Oh he's fine, just a big bump on the head!"

Charlotte ginned. "The joys of parenthood," she replied, sarcastically, reaching for her fries.

Even though she and Tony were roughly the same age, she could never imagine herself with his life – happily married, two young kids, a large semi-detached in a respectable part of the Manchester suburbs. They couldn't be further apart in some respects, and she often wondered if the 'opposites attract' rule is why their friendship worked so well.

Charlotte thought about her own life back at home – her two-bedroomed flat, which had a glorious view of a busy mini-roundabout, a worsening damp problem, and scandalous rental charges. However, the place also had its perks and was the reason she had chosen to live there for as long as she had. These included the absurdly good-looking neighbour upstairs, with whom she would spend the occasional night, amazing acoustics, and the best Chinese takeaway in Salford just a few doors down.

The long line of failed relationships and the ring-free left hand was a flashing beacon to the fact that Charlotte was unmarried. She simply didn't have time to find the perfect husband and, other than the occasional one-night stand, she was happy without a man in her life. Unlike her older sister, Becky, Charlotte didn't have the same urge to conform to society by settling down and having kids and let's face it, she wasn't exactly the marrying type. She was 2 years away from 40 and was old enough and wise enough now to know that marriage and kids were not how it was panning out – and that was fine. She had one love in her life, and her career gave her more pleasure and overall satisfaction than any man could.

Fishing in the brown paper bag for her apple pie, Charlotte removed the cardboard container and pulled out the pastry. Splitting it in two, she popped a piece on a napkin and slid it across the table in Tony's direction. His eyes lit up as he took the small, sugar-filled offering and, in one fluid movement, shoved the whole lot in his mouth.

Charlotte had developed a firm grasp on the workings of a man's brain, and it was true that all of them had a weakness. For some it was sport, some alcohol, for others it was money, and for many it was sex. Tony's weakness, however, was sugar and she had quickly learnt over the 2 years of working together that there was very little he wouldn't do if a Mars bar was wafted enticingly under his nose.

Tony stood to put his empty cup into a nearby bin and, as he was making his way back to the table, his phone vibrated. He reached into his jacket pocket to promptly answer the call.

"Hello, Ma'am." Charlotte stood up in reaction to the faint sound of his boss' voice back in Manchester. Tucking her long hair behind her ears, she tried to hear what Detective Superintendent Anderton was saying to Tony, but the busy restaurant was full of screaming kids who refused to shut up.

"Yes, that's fine Ma'am. Charlotte and I just stopped off at the services for something to eat on the way, so we should be back in Newcastle within the next hour or so… OK, yep, got it, will do. Speak later." Tony ended the call, making his way to the door without further elaboration as Charlotte chased after him.

"What did she want?" asked Charlotte, jogging to keep up with Tony's fast-paced stride. She shoved the food bag into a bin and followed Tony outside to the car park. It was only late afternoon, but it was already starting to get dark, the lights from the motorway vehicles beyond whizzing past in a steady and noisy stream.

"There's more info on the other car that was on the road, the night of Megan's crash," he replied, reaching the car and throwing Charlotte the keys.

"It wasn't a false lead like they thought then?" Charlotte caught the keys effortlessly and jumped into the driver's side.

"Doesn't sound like it."

"The original witness who suggested that Donovan was involved was an unreliable source though?"

"Nope, the witness' story checked out, and there's been more evidence that's come to light."

"So, Emery was right – Rick Donovan's back on the radar?"

Tony reached for his seatbelt and clicked it into place as Charlotte pulled out of the service station car park without even glancing in the mirrors.

Tony usually enjoyed the buzz he got from being right, but had really hoped that on this occasion he would be proved wrong. Stamping his foot impatiently in the foot well, he watched as Charlotte switched on the indicator and pulled onto the motorway heading North towards Newcastle.

"Yep!" Tony eventually replied, his sights set firmly on the road ahead, "Donovan's definitely back on the radar, and it appears that Megan Cooper's crash was no accident."

# Chapter 10

"You all ready to go then?" asks Eva, as she helps me outside with my bags and pops open the boot.

"I think so." I reply, lowering my luggage and surveying her case, which is three times the size of mine. "We're only going away for 2 nights, Eva, Christ you'd think we were going for a month!" I slam the boot as Eva opens the car door.

"A woman can never travel with too many shoes!" she replies, in a half-serious tone.

"It's a tiny fishing village! I think wellies and an anorak will probably be more appropriate attire," I joke.

"I'm not going to pick up a new man dressed like an old fishwife, now am I?" I give a chuckle, but am suddenly on edge as I cross round to the front of the car.

"What've you been doing?" I ask, stopping to bend and inspect a small dent and deep scratch on the bonnet of her 3-month old Audi.

"The driveway gatepost and I had a bit of a scuffle," she responds, laughing, as I climb in next to her and fasten my seatbelt. My heart leaps unexpectedly. It's the first time I've been back in the front seat of a car since the accident and, although I had felt a little apprehensive while I was waiting for Eva to come and pick me up, I didn't anticipate feeling as nervous as I do now.

"Are you alright?" asks Eva, as she pulls away. I've been friends with her since we were 13, and the 17 years that have passed have enabled her the ability to read me like a book.

"Yes, yes, I'm OK," I lie, as I wrap my hand around the seatbelt and grip it firmly.

"We don't have to do this you know, Meg," she replies, pressing on the brake so that the car comes to an abrupt halt in the middle of the road.

"No, really, I want to," I say, untangling my hand from the belt and shifting back in my seat in an attempt to relax. I'm stronger than this – I'm not going to let it beat me.

"Alright then," says Eva, giving me an uncertain glance before she adjusts her rearview mirror to check her make-up, turning to look at me with a bright smile, "Morteford, here we come!"

***

A while later, we arrive in the quaint fishing village of Morteford. Driving down into the village via a steep hill, the appeal of the place is soon apparent. Charming pastel-coloured cottages line the narrow, winding cobbled streets, which lead down to a broad waterfront promenade overlooking a large estuary. The hazy autumn sun reflects off the water, where small fishing boats bob on its calm surface, and the rolling hills of the countryside lie in the far distance; a patchwork design of greens and browns which create a domineering backdrop. We park in a large public car park overlooking the water.

"What a pretty place!" I announce, as I get out of the car and stretch my cramped legs. I take in a deep breath of crisp, fresh air, feeling silently relieved that the long car journey is finally over.

"Yes, it hasn't changed too much from how I remember it," replies Eva, barely glancing up as she pops open the boot and pulls out our cases. "According to the sat nav, the address on that keyring is back that way." She points behind us, towards the main road that we came along to enter the village, "…and our cottage is around here somewhere." She spins around, holding the email that possesses the holiday-home details, as if she's holding a map.

"OK," I answer, "lead the way."

I follow Eva as she passes a play area and small church, towards a heavily cobbled narrow street beyond it. The graveyard at the front of the church is full of ancient-looking stones, and a memorial for the fallen soldiers of World War II has been erected in front of the grounds. I've only been here for 5 minutes, but already I can sense the place is steeped in history. Adjusting the handle on my small case, I lower the wheels to the bumpy ground and clumsily make my way forward to catch up with Eva.

We quickly find the small cottage located at the end of a row of almost identical properties, all with individual coastal themed names. Ours is painted light blue, with a decorative hand-painted picture of a buoy attached to the wall, and it's aptly named 'Fisherman's Retreat sign.' I find myself wondering about the age of the property and how many residents it's had in its time. Births, deaths, loves, losses. If

63

walls could talk I'm sure that this cottage would have many fascinating tales to tell.

Eva fiddles with the lock, using a key provided by the local booking agency, and we let ourselves in to the welcoming cosy space. Just before the door closes behind us, I spin around to look over my shoulder and survey the deserted street beyond.

"What's wrong?" asks Eva, dropping her bag on the floor and joining me back in the doorway.

"Nothing," I reply, shrugging my shoulders as the door clicks shut, and I quickly dismiss the feeling I had. "It's just, I could have sworn someone was behind us."

# Chapter 11

Will was walking along the local docks when Megan arrived in Morteford, and although he felt he'd known she was arriving today, it was a case of pure coincidence that he was in the right place at the right time when they showed up. It didn't take a genius to work out it that was her though; even the car she pulled up in looked totally out of place – far too lavish and ostentatious for a working-class village known more for its beaten-up old trucks and push bikes than top of the range German SUVs with private registration plates.

As soon as he spotted the car entering the village, Will made his way towards it. He had a feeling Megan would be here, though he didn't think it would be quite as soon as this. Reggie – his mother's 8-year-old Golden Retriever – trotted along happily at his side. Holding a red rubber ball in his mouth, he kept looking up at Will, then out to the water, expectantly.

Nearing the car park, he pulled up the hood on his sweatshirt and positioned himself so that he was partially hidden behind a cottage wall where he could clearly make out Megan stretching her legs, as her friend – who he was guessing was Eva due to the number plate of her Audi – pulled something out from the back of the car.

"Shit!" He stamped his foot angrily when he registered the luggage, and Reggie's ears pricked up at the sound as he continued to watch Will. He had hoped it would just be a flying visit when Megan eventually tracked him down, but it looked like she was planning on staying in the village longer than he had anticipated. He only prayed that they weren't going to be here for too long.

Even from a distance, Will could tell that Megan looked well, and he was relieved that she was back on her feet so quickly after the accident. Although it was highly inconvenient that she was now in his hometown, he was grateful for the visible evidence that she was on the mend.

Will followed as the women started to walk away from the car. He needed to know where they were staying so that he could keep track of them while they were here, and he was pleased when, after only a few minutes, they stopped outside a cottage not far from his own.

Megan pulled back her long red hair and held it as the wind picked up strength, and her friend – who looked like she'd walked straight out of a glossy high-fashion magazine – fiddled with the lock on the cottage door. He managed to pivot on the spot and disappear out of view, just before Megan turned to glance at the empty spot where he'd been standing.

Burying his hands in his pockets and breathing down some much-needed heat into the zipped-up collar of his windbreaker, Will picked up his pace towards the ferry landing. Reggie trotted by his side and appeared, rightfully, a little confused by the sudden change in plan which took them away from their regular daily route along the shores of the small bay at the opposite end of the street.

Once at the end of the promenade, and clearly out of view of the cottage they were staying in, Will pulled his phone from his pocket and began to mentally put into action the plan that he had hatched. He wasn't sure how long it would take the ladies to find the address on the keyring and track him down, but he needed to be quick.

For every step they took, Will was going to make absolutely sure that he was always one ahead.

# Chapter 12

"Can everyone come and join us NOW please, I really don't have all day!"

Tony grimaced. Charlotte's tone was as condescending as always when talking to a team she had little to do with on a daily basis. Even after working with her for over 2 years, Tony still felt the overpowering impulse to step in and delicately explain to anyone who didn't personally know Charlotte that her manner was not intended to come across like it did. It was purely due to the passion she had for her job as a detective, and that this case, like all of them, was of massively high importance to her.

Instead, Tony remained silent and decided to leave her to it and let her play her part, just as she had stood back and let Tony take charge an hour ago, when they had arrived back in Newcastle. He made his way to the office, which had been assigned to him while he was working in the area, and closed the door.

Taking a seat on a battered office chair, he studied the photo of Rick Donovan on the desk in front of him, along with his case files from previous years. For a man who was capable of so much, Donovan wasn't significant in any way, shape or form, and Tony found himself wondering again if they had it wrong this time.

***

He had experienced a turbulent past with Rick Donovan, to say the least. He'd been on the crime scene for more years than Tony could care to remember, and the vast majority of his years as a DI in the Northumbria Criminal Investigation Department had been taken up investigating Donovan.

Money laundering, drugs and robbery had been Donovan's forte, but the murders, assaults and trail of destruction that Donovan had always denied involvement in, were the main reason for Tony's involvement. Donovan was well known throughout the North East. A dangerous and insanely clever man, he was the mastermind who pulled the strings of his idiotic puppets, but always managed to remain rooted firmly in the background. He had been in and out of prison over the years, and Tony's crowning glory was being the one to get justice – arresting him after an anonymous tip off, and sending him down for the lengthy, rightfully deserved, sentence.

A few years later, Tony was promoted to a DCI and transferred from Northumbria CID to Manchester, with his family.

Now though, Rick Donovan was out of prison and had been for almost 2 years. He swore to everyone he encountered within the force that he was a changed man – he now had a wealthy wife, and a 6-month-old son. He'd already missed out on his eldest son growing up, Connor, and, as it appeared that he was following in his father's footsteps, he didn't want his youngest to follow suit. From all angles, it seemed that his last stint as a 'model' prisoner had reformed him, and until now, Tony himself had almost believed it.

Donovan had spent the last couple of years lying low, and Tony was unexpectedly shocked when he received the call from his old boss in Newcastle to alert him that a car, fitting the description of Donovan's, had been sighted close to the location of a hit-and-run, which had left a 30-year-old woman trapped in a burning car. He knew that the team here were more than capable of dealing with Donovan; they had, after all, kept a keen eye on him since his release and they were headed up by the best Superintendent Tony had ever encountered in his lengthy career within CID.

However, there was a personal connection with Rick Donovan, which only Tony had. It was one forged from years of watching him, and it was this correlation that had, many times, kept him awake at night, and kept him away from his wife and growing children for too many hours, simply because he wasn't prepared to stop until he finally got justice for what Donovan had done.

He knew Donovan inside out. He understood how his mind worked and what made him tick and, although it meant being away from his family for a little while again now, he had to agree that he was indeed the best person for the job. Also, any case he was involved with would not be complete without Charlotte's steadfast and indefatigable approach to fill any gaps that he happened to miss.

Charlotte was great at her job, and it was clear to Tony that she was well on her way up the career ladder. Her approach wasn't always as proficient as he would like; her professional veneer would often crack and she had a tendency to get too personally involved with the vast majority of their cases and, already, he could see that this one was no exception. Sometimes, though, that passion, and the kind of instinct that simply cannot be taught, is what set her head and shoulders above the rest, figuratively speaking, anyway.

At 5 ft 3 ins in heels, 8 stone dripping wet, and the face of an earthbound angel, Charlotte Taylor's exterior was misleading. She was shit hot at her job and a disgruntled Rottweiler when it came to putting the guilty behind bars. Therefore, when it came to Rick Donovan, Charlotte was just what Tony needed and he was the first to admit that he was lucky when she was assigned to work with him shortly after he arrived in Manchester 2 years ago. Although he dearly missed living in the North East, he didn't have any regrets, yet.

There was a knock on the door and Tony looked up to see his old boss and still-close friend, Detective Superintendent Joe Emery, popping his head round. He had known him for years and Joe had even been one of his ushers when he and Olivia were married 12 years ago.

Joe had been working in CID for more years than Tony could recall and now, as he approached 60, the man was showing no signs of slowing down. He had been here from day one, when Tony started working for the department almost 14 years ago, as an ambitious and overly enthusiastic young DC, and he had become both a role-model superior and a close friend to Tony and his family over the years.

Emery was a good guy who he missed the most after relocating to Manchester, and it was because of Emery that

Tony was now back in the North East helping out. After returning yesterday, Tony had quickly realized that there were no longer many faces he recognized here, and seeing Joe again today had made him feel at home, as he always used to.

"Settling in alright, Tone?" Joe asked, in the same heavy Glaswegian accent that had taken Tony many months to decrypt, back when they had first met. The 30 odd years that Joe had lived in the North East had not even slightly softened the heavy Scottish accent.

"Yeah, great cheers, Joe." Tony moved a large pile of papers to one side. "Feels like I've never been away."

"Yes, can't deny, things haven't really been the same without you around here these past couple of years. A lot quieter for one!"

Tony smiled.

"How's the job treating you down in Manchester then?" asked Emery.

"Yeah, not bad. I've inherited a great team so can't complain. Still miss CID, though to be honest."

"Not quite the 'Life on Mars' experience that you had imagined, then?"

Tony smirked, "Not quite."

"Ah, don't take it to heart Tone. You're bloody good at your job, but let's face it, you're no Gene Hunt."

Tony laughed and nodded in agreement.

"If you hadn't noticed, I'm a bit light on the floor here, if you ever fancied coming back? You know I'd always keep the door open for you." Joe winked.

"You know me Joe, never say never."

"That's good to know, Tony." Joe pointed through the glass panels of the office door behind him. "That DI of yours is a lot to handle, isn't she?"

"Charlotte? Nah, she's alright once you get to know her, Joe – I promise."

Joe nodded and took another quick glance at Charlotte, who had finished her briefing and was now talking to one of the department's new detective constables; a tall woman with short, cropped ginger hair. Tony briefly wondered if the poor girl knew what she was letting herself in for.

"I'll take your word for it," replied Joe, clearly unconvinced that Charlotte wasn't as bad as she appeared. "Fancy getting together for a pint later? It would be good to catch up."

"Yeah, sounds good, mate. I'll give you a bell when I finish up here."

Joe gave a thumbs up and stepped back out into the corridor, letting the office door close. Before it did, Tony caught sight of Charlotte again who was now pacing back and forth with her hands on her hips, something she did a lot when she was pondering. He observed a couple of young PCSOs sauntering past, clearly checking her out, and he chuckled when she stopped pacing and mouthed a jokey "piss off" in their direction.

His attention now back to the task at hand, Tony sat forward and continued to skim through all of the old case files bearing Rick Donovan's name, which were scattered out on the desk in front of him; many included reports from past years, with his own handwriting.

He sighed, knowing that he didn't need to read any further and that no more research was required; Donovan's history was as visible in Tony's mind as his own. Putting his hands behind his head, Tony leaned back in his seat, eyes fixing on a dark water stain on the ceiling. His instincts around Donovan had never been wrong before, and he didn't know if it was just the amount of time that had passed without him encountering Donovan, or just the fact that he was beginning to ever-so-slightly lose his touch, but he couldn't help thinking that something wasn't quite right; it felt different.

Tony had an overwhelming feeling that this time he was missing something, but for now, he couldn't put his finger on it.

# Chapter 13

I step out of the cottage and draw in a lung full of fresh sea air. Even though numerous times since arriving in Morteford, I had questioned us coming here, I am now really pleased that we did. It feels good to be away from home for a short time and, after only a few hours, I feel a weight lifting from my shoulders; it's clear to me how much I really needed this break.

"I'll catch you up," shouts Eva from inside the cottage. I click open the front door and glance back at her in the living room, where she holds her mobile in the air. "I'm just going to call Maisie."

"Tell her Auntie Megan says 'hi'," I shout back, before I step out into the dimly lit street.

I smile to myself as I start a slow stroll towards the promenade, thinking of my gorgeous niece back at home. Maisie is the apple of Eva's eye, and although her parents are no longer together, Eva and Steve dote on the 6-year-old; as do I. So did Johnny.

My thoughts turn to my late husband as I continue walking, just as they have every day in the year since he died. It doesn't surprise me one bit that he enjoyed holidays here so much when he was younger; he must have loved it. Although he had mentioned Morteford a few times in passing, on seeing it for the first time, I am shocked that in the 9 years we were together he had never brought me here. On first impressions, it's clear to see the village is a special place and already, I find myself liking it.

I continue along the street towards the promenade at the end and pass dog walkers, smiling courteously as they make their way to the water's edge. It's freezing cold and starting to get dark, even though it's just gone teatime and it's a brutal reminder that the winter months will soon be upon us.

I dig out a pair of gloves from the depths of my coat pocket and slip my hands into the warm wool, then stop at Eva's car to wait for her to catch up. She thinks that the address we want is on the way back out of the village, so we have decided to walk there. Even though it's cold, taking the car may be a waste of time due to the number of narrow traffic-free streets. We could have waited until morning to find the address, but curiosity is playing havoc and I can't wait. I want to find the man who saved my life!

I wait a few more minutes before Eva finally comes into view at the bottom of the street and makes her way over to me in the car park.

"Sorry about that," she says. Steve wanted a quick chat with me."

"How's Maisie doing?" I ask, as we continue walking.

"She's great," replies Eva. She zips up her pink bomber jacket, pulls the fur-trimmed hood up over her long blonde hair, and digs her hands deep into her pockets. "It'll do them both good to spend some time together."

I nod. Eva and Steve aren't on what you would call 'friendly terms' anymore. They simply tolerate one another for Maisie's sake. However, Eva would be the first to admit that the one thing she can't knock her ex on is his parenting skills. He's been a brilliant dad to Maisie since the day she was born, and probably a much better aunt than I have been recently. I haven't seen Maisie for a few weeks, mainly due to the amount of time I have been spending at work, and then the accident.

We continue to walk in silence and have made it to the end of the promenade in less than 15 minutes. I've counted only a handful of shops, pubs and cafes by the time we round the corner and we luckily encounter a sign bearing the street name printed on the keyring.

"It must be along this road somewhere," says Eva, squinting against a rush of icy cold air towards a long uphill street in front of us. She looks down at her high-heeled boots uncertainly.

"Told you that you should have brought flats!" I say, as I begin the steep climb. "I've brought a couple of pairs – you could have borrowed them if your feet weren't double the size of mine."

"Just going to have to brave it," replies Eva, beginning the climb.

We are both out of breath and struggling by the time we reach the top of the hill, clearly not as fit as we would like to believe. Soon the road ends so we can't go any further and I stop when we reach a large building, which looks as if it could have been a stately home in its former years.

"This is it!" I announce, as Eva joins me at the gates.

"It couldn't have been at the bottom of the flippin' hill, could it?", she says breathlessly

"Oh, stop moaning."

"What number did you say it was?" asks Eva. She opens the black, iron gate, which creaks on its rusted hinges, and we make our way to the main entrance of the building, where steps lead up to a large wooden porch. There's only one light on, which seems to be coming from the back of the property. The grounds are probably beautiful in the daylight, filled with trees, and beyond them, the calm water of the estuary is lit by moonlight.

"Apartment three," I reply.

A nervous sensation hits the pit of my stomach as I join Eva on the steps. She presses the number three buzzer, but there's no reply.

"Come on Eva, there's nobody at home," I say, as she waits a few seconds, then presses the buzzer impatiently.

"Come on!" I repeat, "we'll try again tomorrow." I grab her arm to pull her away, but as we reach the bottom step, the door behind us opens and I turn to see a middle-aged woman in the doorway.

"Can I help you?" she asks, clearly angry.

"Yes!" says Eva, assertively. I hang back as she makes her way back up the steps closer to the woman.

"We're looking for the man who lives in apartment number three," she says.

The woman looks puzzled.

"Apartment three hasn't had anyone in it for a while," she replies, giving Eva an unsure glance, followed by a full inspection.

"Oh," says Eva, "It's just that we found a key to the apartment and wanted to return it."

The woman tuts and shakes her head. "What's he like?" she announces, more to herself than to us. "He's forever losing that sodding key."

"I thought you said the apartment was empty?" I say, joining Eva in front of the woman. Her patchouli-scented perfume hits me – the smell is almost overpowering.

"Yes, it is, but there's a man busy renovating it," she replies in a credulous tone, implying that we are stupid. "He's here every day, checking the workmen who are carrying out the renovations." She holds out her hand to me. "He'll be needing that key back so I'll pass it onto him if you want."

I reach to take the key out of my pocket, but Eva puts up her hand to stop me.

"We'd rather pass it on to him ourselves," she says, "he helped my friend out recently and she would like to meet him to say thank you."

The woman visibly scowls at me, clearly understanding that she is going to have to provide more than she already has if Eva and I are to leave her in peace.

"His name's Will Travers! He and another bloke run a property company based over the other side of the estuary, in Fadstow."

"Fadstow? How do we get over there?" asks Eva.

"There's a ferry that runs every half an hour from Morteford Docks. That's the fastest way to get there." The woman glances at her watch. "Hmm, the last one was at 6 o'clock so you've missed it."

"Oh, OK, thanks," replies Eva, cynically.

"It's Friday night though," adds the woman, as Eva and I turn away from her.

"Pardon?"

"Will drinks in the Anchor. It's down on the waterfront and you'll probably find him in there tonight."

"Oh, great thank you for letting us know," I reply.

The woman half smiles and slams the door.

# Chapter 14

The Anchor Tavern's was what my neck of the woods would refer to as 'a total dive'. With heavy, wooden, old-fashioned furniture and a bar full of cask ales, it seems to appeal to a predominantly male crowd.

Eva glowers as we enter.

"Nice place," she says, sarcastically. If there was ever an opportunity for Eva to drop the snobbery in her, now would be it, but tonight, I don't hold out much hope.

She puts her hands on her hips and plants her feet, eyeing the crowds of men in front of her incredulously.

"Come on Eva," I plead. "We only have to stay for a few drinks – I just want to see if Will Travers shows up," I shout to her over the live band playing loud folk music.

Eva rolls her eyes in my direction.

"OK, but we're not staying here all night!" she replies, turning her back on me and winding her way through the crowds in the direction of the bar. I follow, sticking closely behind her and pushing past the punters, 80% of them male. I can feel eyes studying us, the testosterone almost palpable as I continue through to the back of the pub where a large, open fire begins to work its magic and thaw me out following the walk back from the apartments. Although it had been freezing, it had been a damn sight easier trekking back down the hill.

"What can I get you?" asks the guy behind the bar, sporting a thick grey beard and dark features.

"White wine, please," I mouth to Eva, over the rowdy punters. Eva nods and shouts "Can I have a white wine and a Mojito please?"

The barman smirks at Eva and stifles a laugh in my direction – I smile back apologetically.

"I don't think this is a 'Mojito' type of place, do you Eva?" I whisper in her ear.

For an intelligent woman, who finished at the top of her class at university and went on to be a successful businesswoman, Eva certainly has the dumb-blonde charade off to a tee.

"Oh, OK then, what do you recommend?" she asks the barman, appearing only mildly embarrassed.

"We do some nice local ciders," he replies, kindly.

"OK, I'll try one of them thanks," answers Eva. She catches the eye of a good-looking blonde man of around our age who's sitting on a bar stool next to her and, giving him a flirtatious smile, she straightens her sequin-studded jumper over her ample cleavage, handing over the money for our drinks.

"I don't suppose you know a man called Will Travers?" I ask the barman, steadying myself as a woman pushes roughly past me.

"Will? Yes, he's a regular, love."

"Is he here tonight?

The barman has a quick glance around before replying. "No, he's not, although he's usually in every Friday night at some point with his mate, Elliott." The barman looks down at his watch. "They're normally in by now, so I presume they're not coming tonight, but if they show up later, I'll let you know." He gives me a warm smile.

"Thank you," I answer, before taking my drink from Eva and moving her away from the guy at the bar towards two strangely empty seats at the back of the pub, near the fire.

\*\*\*

Will Travers didn't show up last night – we stayed at the Anchor until closing time, but he and his friend never arrived. I'm now heading over to Fadstow because Mike – the owner of the pub – assured me that Will would be working in the office this morning.

"You sure you're alright getting the ferry over there on your own?" asks Eva. She pulls her fluffy dressing gown around her and shivers, reaching up to fiddle with the thermostat on the living-room wall of the cottage before finally admitting defeat and heading over to start the open fire.

"I'll be fine!" I answer, "I'll just pop over there to return his key and say thank you, then I'll come back and we can go for lunch together, somewhere nice."

"Yeah, I think I could do with something to soak up the alcohol from last night," replies Eva. Stretching out on the large, comfy sofa in the living room, she rubs her head. "I'm dying."

"That's what happens when you get carried away with the local brew," I joke, playing along with what we both know is nothing more than a poor excuse. Eva's hangover isn't the main reason she isn't accompanying me today; it's because I have to get a ferry over the water to Fadstow and deep water is something she has been terrified of since Johnny died.

"See you later then," I say. Eva nods and gives a wry smile, as if silently thanking me for not pushing her to join me.

"See you later, Meg," she replies quietly.

\*\*\*

The walk to the ferry landing takes 10 minutes and I only have to wait a further five for the small boat to dock near the narrow wooden jetty where a few people, beside myself, are waiting in a short queue to board.

A man helps me onto the small boat and I take a seat at the back with the other passengers; another crew member runs through a few safety instructions, before the skipper fires up the boat's engine and we begin the ride over to Fadstow.

The sun is rising above the estuary as we continue the short trip across the water. Looking back towards Morteford, I can't quite believe how beautiful it looks this morning, with its deserted streets and warm orange glow of the rising sun, contrasted against the washed-out colours of the old fishermen's cottages. The water shimmers against the low light and, as I sit back to relax and enjoy the journey, I can't help thinking about Eva and how much she would have loved this, before the accident and her phobia of water developed. The day that Johnny died.

Johnny and Eva had been staying with their parents at their villa in the South of Spain when it happened; the day all of our lives were ripped apart and changed forever. Eva had just been through a bad break-up with Steve, and had decided to take Maisie over to Spain to escape for a long weekend and get away from it all. Johnny went with them, and I was going out to meet them the following day because I had an important last-minute business conference that I couldn't miss.

The day of my arrival, Eva and Johnny had taken Maisie to the beach, and Johnny was due to pick me up from the airport later that afternoon. Not many people knew about the quiet cove near to the holiday home. I'd been there numerous times with Johnny in the 9 years that we had been together, and it's the spot where he proposed to me. It was deserted then too.

Eva and Maisie were playing in the sea when they got into trouble. Johnny succeeded to pull Maisie to safety, and he then swam back out to rescue Eva. He managed to get her to shallower water where she was able to regain control, away from the current that had taken hold. Johnny wasn't so lucky and was swept out with it. I was on the plane bound for Spain, 35,000 feet in the air, when it all happened. I was later greeted at the airport by Eva and Johnny's distraught parents, telling me that their son was missing. After 2 days of relentless searching by the Spanish authorities, Johnny was certified dead and my world crumbled beneath me.

"Are you ready, Miss?" My thoughts are interrupted as the ferry's skipper taps me on the shoulder. I glance around and realize that the boat has now come to a halt on the opposite side of the estuary, and the other passengers have already disembarked.

"Oh, yes, sorry!" I reply, quickly rising from my seat. The man helps me across the small gap between the bobbing boat and the jetty. I smile and thank him, politely.

"Could you tell me where A.W.E. renovations is based please?" I ask the man, before he jumps back down onto the deck of the boat. Mike, from the pub, had told me the name of Will Travers' company. Apparently it's named after Will, his business partner, and Will's father, who once ran the company, before handing it over to him after discovering he was ill a couple of years ago. Mike had told me that Will renamed the company following the takeover, to ensure his father's name was incorporated; a gesture I thought very touching. Even though I'm yet to meet Will Travers, I find I'm already growing fond of him.

"Yes miss, it's that big building with the red door, at the far end there." The skipper points to the end of the street where I can see a large building up a small bank, overlooking the water.

"Thanks very much." I reply, before starting the short walk.

I make it to the office as it starts to rain. Scolding myself for not bringing an umbrella, I race to take cover under the door's porch. I try the handle, but it doesn't budge and I'm starting to think that I've wasted my time when the door swings open with so much force that I almost fall through it.

"Can I help?" asks a tall, well-built man with short-cropped, dark hair and wearing a smart, navy suit. I know instantly – it's him!

"Hi, I, I—" For some reason, I've forgotten how to speak and I stammer before pulling myself together. "I'm, erm, looking for someone. Actually, I think it might be you!" My cheeks are burning with embarrassment.

The man stares back at me vacantly.

"Are you Will Travers?"

"Yes."

I nod and take a step closer to him, holding out my hand, "I'm Megan Cooper." Will shakes it gently.

"You might not remember me," I continue.

Will's silence confirms my suspicions that he has no clue who I am.

"I was in a car accident last week, up near Newcastle, and you helped me," I continue.

There's a sharp glint in Will's eyes as the realization hits him.

"Oh, yes, of course. I'm really glad you're OK, Megan." His tone seems flat – there's no emotion at all in his voice, and I suddenly feel ridiculous for tracking him down. There are a few seconds of awkward silence before I remember why I'm actually standing outside his office.

"Oh, sorry," I reach into my handbag and remove the key. "I think this is yours?" I hold it out to him.

Will continues to look unimpressed, adding to my feeling of foolishness.

"You came all the way here to give me this?" taking the key from me, his expression turns to quizzical.

"Yes," I reply. "And I wanted to say thank you. If it hadn't been for you showing up like that, I would be dead. You saved my life!"

Will shifts his weight and rubs at his unshaven chin.

"You're welcome," he says quietly, looking down at the ground.

"You left your jacket behind, that's how I found the key, but I had to throw the jacket away because it was very badly...scorched." The police still have the jacket in their possession and Will doesn't need to know that; however, I'm not sure why I feel the need to lie.

"I can buy you a new one? I know they're expensive." I dig into my handbag to pull out my cheque book, but Will reaches out to touch my arm and stops me in my tracks. I look at him properly for the first time and our eyes meet.

"No, you don't need to do that. It was just an old coat." His stare holds mine. His eyes are huge and almost as blue as the water in front of us.

"Oh, OK, if you're sure!" I take a step back, feeling awkward, but not insisting he takes the money. Judging by the sports car parked by the door, and the fact that he could afford a coat that probably cost him in excess of £700, I doubt he needs reimbursement.

"Well, thanks for returning this, Megan." He holds up the key and slips it into his suit pocket; I nod, taking that as a hint that our conversation is over.

"Thank you for saving my life!" I respond, flatly. I begin to back away from the shelter of the doorway and out into the heavy rain.

"Any time," Will smiles briefly, before the door closes.

# Chapter 15

I'm soaked through and feeling really fed up by the time I get back to the cottage. Eva, still in the same nightwear I left her in an hour ago, jumps up from the sofa as soon as I enter the living room.

"Christ, you're absolutely drenched!" she exclaims, stating the obvious. She takes my wet coat and I squeeze the rainwater from my dripping hair before I fall heavily onto the sofa. Eva moves to the open fire and, from a wicker basket, throws some more kindling onto it before she sits back down.

"So, what happened?" she asks, pushing a stray blonde curl behind her ear and tucking one foot beneath her.

"Oh, not much really" I reply, as casually as I can. "Went to his office, gave him his key, I said 'thank you' and he said 'you're welcome'."

"And that's it? No explanation of why he was in the North East last week?"

"Nope."

"And he didn't give you a reason for not giving his name, or coming to the hospital?"

"No."

"You didn't talk?"

"No, the conversation was over before it began really."

"That's a bit strange!"

I remove my boots and socks, trying to regain the circulation in my frozen feet.

"Yep."

"So, you really didn't have *any* sort of chat with him?" Eva continues to throw questions at me.

"He didn't exactly seem the chatty type, Eva." I say, a little irritated by the constant stream of questions being thrown at me as I'm barely through the door.

"And he didn't even invite you in from the rain?"

"No, he bloody didn't! Hence why I am now like a drowned rat." I gesture towards my soaked jeans and limp wet hair.

Eva smiles and reaches over to rub my arm affectionately.

"Sorry, Meg – I know you'd hoped for some answers today."

I suddenly have a deep feeling of dissatisfaction and I can't really explain why. What was I hoping for when I finally met this man? Had I really been expecting anything other than the reaction I got? I can't deny that he's all I have thought about since the accident, and, in a strange sort of way, I know that I have developed a kind of fascination with this stranger who saved my life. After meeting him this morning, however, I feel utterly disappointed.

"Well, I'm feeling a lot better now," says Eva. "Why don't we go and get some lunch somewhere nice. My treat?"

"Sounds like a plan," I reply, rising to my feet again. "I'll just go and grab a shower and get changed."

I hear Eva's phone ringing as I dry my hair, but I can't make out the conversation through the wall of the cottage, only her muffled voice. A moment later she has a huge, excited grin on her face when she pops her head around the bedroom door.

"What's up?" I ask as I open my make-up bag and begin rubbing moisturizer into my cheeks.

"That was the lad I met in the pub last night," she replies, brightly.

"Who?" I laugh, "you mean, that Jack guy you were talking to at the bar for barely a few minutes? I didn't even realize you'd given him your number!"

Eva nods proudly, "he's asked me out for a few drinks and lunch today."

"That's brilliant, Eva!" I reply, smiling.

"Do you honestly not mind though Meg? I know I said we'd go out today, and I feel guilty for leaving you, but he was…"

"Gorgeous! Yes, I know, and don't be silly. I'm a big girl and can occupy myself for a few hours. Get out there and have some fun."

"I know, but I came here to keep you company after all."

"It's fine, honest. It's stopped raining now anyway so I'll have a walk and take a look around the village. I spotted a little art museum earlier, so I might visit that."

Eva scrunches her nose. Although my idea of a good day out involves learning and culture, it couldn't be further from what Eva enjoys. Jack has given her the perfect excuse to avoid being dragged round an art museum while I admire the paintings and give her a running commentary of something she has absolutely no interest in.

"Thanks a lot, Meg," Eva beams at me, "I promise we'll go out tonight and spend tomorrow morning together before we head home," she adds, before she leaves to get ready for her lunch date.

***

The sun is shining again, and the earlier cloudy sky has given way to a bright and clear afternoon, as I make my way to the village centre. Adjusting my woollen scarf against the bite of the coastal breeze, I keep a slow pace. The village remains as relaxed as it was when we arrived yesterday, with only a few weekend tourists peering into the small gift shops, and the odd local dog walker wandering along the narrow maze of cobbled lanes. I decide to treat myself to fish and chips and, sitting on a nearby bench overlooking the water, I unwrap the paper. The smell of vinegar hits me full force and, as the heat rises up to thaw my cold face, I dig in hungrily.

It's only when I spot an old couple walking hand-in-hand along the path in front of me that loneliness strikes. The emotion doesn't rise from the fact that Eva isn't with me and I'm in a place I'm not familiar with. I'm an independent woman and always have been; doing my own thing comes naturally to me and I've stood on my own two feet from a young age. When I lost my mum at 19, it reinforced how self-sufficient I actually am. I climbed the career ladder at work, gaining a respectable position within one of the largest retail firms in the country.

On a day-to-day basis I keep busy, so that the feelings of loneliness are kept at a manageable level. However, it's times like these, when I let my barriers down for a few seconds, that the pain returns and I'm cruelly reminded that I am, after all, a widow and I'll never again share special moments with the man I truly loved.

Feeding the seagulls a handful of battered fish, and throwing the remainder of my lunch into a nearby bin, I head towards the museum I'd spotted earlier, located near the ferry landing. I'm grateful for the warmth as I enter – I'm still frozen from the soaking I received earlier and I doubt I'll thaw out properly before the day is through. I decide to grab a coffee in the café before I look around.

I join the small queue and, as I'm nearing the front, I realize the man standing in front of me is Will Travers. Feeling the same awkwardness I had on our earlier meeting, I decide to avoid another encounter with him and turn to walk away. However, as I do, I catch my elbow on the corner of a container full of cutlery and it crashes noisily to the floor. Will bends down to help me clear up the mess and only acknowledges who I am when we are crouched on the floor at eye level.

"Oh hi, Megan, isn't it?" he asks, a smile forming and then quickly fading to the expression of non-emotion he'd had earlier.

I nod, as I place the last of the cutlery into the plastic container he's holding and we stand back up.

"Yes, it is. Hello again, Will."

"That will be £2.80," interrupts the young girl behind the counter, handing Will a small cup of coffee.

"Please, let me." I thrust a £10 note into the girl's hand before Will has the chance to protest, "and I'll have a latte, please." I smile, and the girl turns away to prepare it.

"Thank you!" says Will, taking the cup and cradling it in his hands.

"It's the least I can do," I reply. The girl behind the counter hands me my drink and change, and I turn to leave.

"Erm, Megan, would you like to join me?" I spin on my heel, surprised, and meet his eye.

"Yes, that would be nice!" I respond.

I follow him to a window seat overlooking the estuary, and I briefly wonder if there are many buildings in this village that don't boast a picturesque view.

"So, you're staying here in Morteford?" asks Will casually. He lifts his mug of coffee, blows on it, and takes a sip.

"Yes," I reply, "my friend and I are staying in a holiday cottage just down the road."

Will nods in acknowledgement. "Will you be here for long?"

"No, we go home tomorrow."

"So you came all the way here just to return my key?" Will sounds sceptical, and I'm not surprised. My actions do seem a little eccentric.

"And to say thank you, yes." Once again, I feel a sense of embarrassment and totally removed from the woman who stands up to present in front of a crowded room of patronizing businessmen, able to put them in their place at the drop of a hat.

Will looks out over the estuary, thoughtfully.

"So, where's your friend today?"

"Eva? Oh she met a guy in the Anchor Tavern last night and he invited her out for lunch this afternoon."

Will smiles. "The Anchor, eh? I regularly drink in there."

"Yes, I know, we were waiting for you last night – the lady at the place you're renovating said you might be there."

"Aaah, so that's how you found out where I work?" The penny drops.

"Yes." I smile.

"What's the name of the guy your friend has gone out with?"

"Jack something or other."

"Oh, that'll be Jack Dalton! Nice guy, but not like him to have the guts to do something like that – he's usually pretty shy around women, so must have taken the chance! The local men aren't used to seeing beautiful women like yourself."

I blush, and on realizing what he's just said, Will quickly changes the subject.

"Are you recovered now then, after the accident?" He fiddles with a loose thread dangling from the sleeve of his jumper.

"Yes, I'm fine thanks. I was in hospital for a couple of days though, so they could keep an eye on me."

"Before they took you in the ambulance, the paramedics said that your injuries weren't too serious."

"Yes, just a little smoke inhalation and a few cuts and bruises, but they said I'm lucky to be alive."

Will looks back out over the water and sighs.

"I'm really sorry I couldn't come with you, but I had a flight to catch. I was on my way to the airport when I saw your car at the bottom of the ravine."

"Were you on business in the area?" I grab the chance to find out the real reason he was away from home.

"Yes – my business partner and I have some clients based near Newcastle. I was just meeting up with them, then returning here to pass on the details to Elliott. I felt terrible leaving you like that, but, like I say, the paramedics said you were OK and I was running late to drop off the hire car and catch the last flight home."

I nod, but wonder if, in his position, I would have hung around longer.

"It's OK, I totally understand," I lie. "I'm just grateful you were passing by when you did."

"How did the accident happen anyway?" asks Will. "Can you remember anything about it?"

I shudder – reliving the memory is a daily, and ongoing, struggle.

"There was a car coming towards me so I swerved to miss it and went off the road."

"There was another car?!" Will seems shocked. "I didn't see another car."

"You wouldn't have! It was long gone by the time you got there, and the police think it was kids joyriding."

"And they didn't stop to see if you were OK?"

"No, the police reckon they were probably too scared to stop and were half expecting they'd hand themselves in, but I'm not sure they'll come forward voluntarily now."

"If they have any sort of decency, or a conscience, then you shouldn't have to wait too long."

"No, maybe not. I haven't heard anything though so I'm presuming they're still looking into it." I pick up my mug, take a sip of the still-hot coffee and again think back to the visit from the detectives earlier in the week.

"I hope they catch them," says Will softly.

"Yeah, me too."

"Did you tell the police that you were coming here to find me?"

"No, I didn't really think they needed to know; besides, I decided to come here after I'd spoken to them."

Will nods and I spot what I think is a fleeting look of relief.

I'm draining the last of my coffee when my mobile rings, and, when I reach into my bag expecting it to be Eva, the display shows a number I don't recognize.

"Hello, Megan Cooper speaking."

"Megan, hi, it's DCI Morgan." His authoritative, thick Geordie accent rings loudly in my ear.

"Oh, hello, how can I help you?" I ask, feeling the anxiety bubble to the surface.

"DI Taylor and I popped round to see you today, but you weren't home. Your brother, Luke isn't it, told us you're away for the weekend?"

"Yes, due back tomorrow."

"That's good as we need to speak to you again. Can you call us as soon as you return please?"

"Yes, course, but what's this all about?"

"Nothing to worry about and everything's under control – just a few things we need to ask you."

"Oh alright. I'll call you tomorrow."

"Great, thanks Megan. Speak to you then."

I hang up on DCI Morgan and look back at Will.

"Everything alright?" he asks.

"Yes, well I think so. The police want to talk to me when I get home."

"About the accident presumably?"

"Yes, although he didn't say."

"Maybe they've found the kids who were driving the car?"

"Yeah, maybe."

I reach for my coat and stand up, not really feeling in the mood to look around the gallery.

"I think I'll head back to the cottage now." I push back my seat, and, as I stand, so does Will.

"I'll walk back with you if that's OK? I'm meeting Elliott in the Anchor soon."

I nod, but am not really listening. There was something about DCI Morgan's tone that has made me nervous, and I start to think that this whole mess isn't over yet and that, possibly, it's only just begun.

# Chapter 16

Charlotte closed the hotel door behind her and slumped down heavily onto the perfectly made, king-sized bed. It had been a bloody gruelling day! Nevertheless, she knew that they were getting closer to the truth, and that it was only a matter of time before the answers they wanted would be revealed. She switched on the TV and glanced at her watch; it was almost 8.30 pm and she said she'd meet Tony downstairs in the restaurant at 9 o'clock, so she'd better get a move on.

Grabbing a quick shower to wake herself up, she threw on a pair of skinny jeans and an oversized jumper, and searched for a hairdryer. After a few frenzied moments of pulling open every drawer and cupboard in the room, she came to the conclusion that she'd have to do without, so, giving her long hair a quick towel dry, she left the room and headed for the nearest lift.

The hotel was a decent one actually – far better than some of the hovels she and Tony had stayed in on the rare occasion they were away from base. She knew that Tony's old boss, Joe Emery, had a lot to do with it, like when he'd pulled strings to grant permission for her and Tony to work in Newcastle. She also suspected that he had helped foot the bill for their stay. She could tell that Emery wanted Tony back in Newcastle on a more permanent basis, and to convince him to return, bribery was the first card he pulled from his pack!

Tony was already seated at a table when Charlotte arrived at the restaurant. He had his mobile in his hand and, although she liked to believe he was having some chill time with a game or a brain teaser, she knew whatever he was doing would be work related and that even if he did fancy playing a game to pass the time, he was totally incapable of downloading one! A self-confessed technophobe, Tony had only recently given in to modern technology by finally owning an iPhone, thereby dragging himself kicking and screaming into the 21st century.

"Hi honey, you miss me?" she asked, pulling up a chair and wasting no time in studying the nearest menu.

"Oh these 40 minutes apart have been excruciating!" exclaimed Tony, not even glancing up from his mobile.

"You ordered yet?"

"No, I thought I'd be a gent and wait for you, although I could eat the table cloth I'm so bloody hungry!" Tony glanced up from his phone. "Christ almighty, what have you come as? Has there been a flood in your room?"

"Ha-ha, you're hilarious!" Charlotte ruffled her damp hair. "There's no hairdryer in my room – what sort of 4-star hotel doesn't have a hairdryer these days?"

"Quite a few, actually," replied Tony, matter-of-factly, before picking up a second menu. His eyes trailed over the trendy and overpriced options. Nearly 15 quid for a burger?! All he really wanted was a home-cooked roast, but he knew he would have no luck getting that until he arrived home. Liv made the best roast beef and Yorkshire puddings he had ever tasted, and no restaurant food, however swanky, would come close.

"Hell of a day, eh?" asked Charlotte.

Tony snapped the menu shut after hardly looking at it.

"Yep."

A waitress appeared, casually flirting with Tony as she took their order, and Charlotte wanted to tell the poor girl that she was wasting her time. Tony was strictly a one-woman man, and the love he and his wife had for each other was pretty nauseating most of the time. Instead, she chose to sit back and watch as the waitress mildly humiliated herself in front of a man completely oblivious to her advances.

Not that Charlotte had ever tried her luck with Tony. Even if he hadn't been married when they met, she knew where she stood from day one, and, although a decent enough looking guy, he was far too powerful a presence for her. She liked to be in control in a relationship and she knew that would never be the case with Tony, however, even though technically speaking he was her boss, they saw each other as equals, and their relationship had always, and would always, be purely platonic.

"Come on Char, what you having?"

Charlotte snapped back into action and looked up at the waitress.

"Sorry, I'll have the steak, medium rare, with chips, and a very large vodka and tonic please." She closed her menu and smiled at Tony, who returned a less-than-impressed look.

"Coke, I'll have a Coke." She amended her order under her boss' glare. Tony shook his head and chuckled, before ordering a lemonade and a chicken curry.

"Have you spoken to Megan Cooper again yet?" Charlotte asked. They had managed almost 15 minutes before the conversation turned to work; actually a personal best for them!

"I called her earlier – she gets back tomorrow afternoon so we can go and see her then," Tony replied.

The waitress returned, first placing Tony's drink down before flashing him a smile through newly glossed lips.

"Cheers!" he said to the waitress, and without a second glance, plucked the slice of lime from his drink, throwing it clumsily into Charlotte's glass.

Charlotte ignored what, in Tony's world, would be a gallant gesture.

"Where's she been then?"

"I spoke to her brother, Luke, this morning. He told me she'd gone down to Morteford for the weekend, with her sister-in-law."

"Morteford? Why, what's there?"

Tony shrugged. "Beats me! I told her to call us as soon as she gets home."

Charlotte nodded.

"I'm surprised she wants to go anywhere so soon after that horrible crash." She picked up her Coke and took a sip through the copious amount of floating citrus fruit.

"Me too," replied Tony. "Although I suppose she just wanted to get away from it all for a bit and in a way I can see where she's coming from."

"Yeah, maybe. It's nice to get away and recharge the batteries sometimes – I can't remember when I last did that."

Tony placed his mobile on the table. A picture of his wife and kids was displayed on its screensaver. His daughter had his dark eyes, his son the same delicate features as his wife, Olivia. Tony's eyes lingered on their faces until the screen went dark.

"No, me neither Charlotte."

\*\*\*

They were finishing their meals when his phone vibrated its way across the table, and he pounced on it with lightning-quick reflexes. Charlotte pulled her still-damp hair into a ponytail and secured it with a band, calling the waitress over for the bill. She knew that any call at this time in the evening was usually attached to a work-related matter, rather than Tony's wife calling to feed him the latest update from the Morgan clan.

"DCI Morgan. Hi Joe… yep… no problem, we're on our way – be there in 20."

Charlotte picked up a napkin and dabbed the side of her mouth, then reached for her handbag as Tony drained the last of his lemonade and set his empty glass down.

"Emery's called us in."

"I guessed that bit Tony, what's up?"

"Rick Donovan's finally started talking."

"At last!"

Tony made his way out of the restaurant, across the hotel lobby, and out of the revolving doors. Jogging down the hotel steps, he stopped to wait for Charlotte to catch up after she'd gone to retrieve her coat; a sensible move on her part. Wearing only a thin t-shirt, Tony was already feeling numb.

Charlotte made her way to where he was casually leaning against some railings with his back to the quayside – the mysterious waters of the River Tyne and its notorious bridges boasting their full splendor behind him. Although Tony had seen Newcastle many times, and it no longer had a profound effect on him, Charlotte appreciated the view, slowing her pace slightly to absorb the atmosphere. The quayside was bustling and alive with people beginning their Saturday nights in the many pubs and restaurants that the city had to offer.

Making their way along the quayside towards the car park, Charlotte fastened her coat and loosened her now almost-dry hair. A group of half-drunk men, seemingly on a stag do and dressed as ballerinas, wolf whistled as she passed. Tony stopped abruptly and, as they continued along the path muttering laddish obscenities to each other, he shot them down with a potent stare. The men were instantly quiet!

Tony didn't look like a stereotypical DCI tonight. Dressed in casual jeans and a t-shirt, which revealed the tip of a large tattoo covering the whole of his left shoulder, he appeared like any other local bloke. Nevertheless, there was something about his presence that silently encouraged other men to back down.

Charlotte grinned and picked up her pace towards him. She knew that Tony was fully aware of her ability to handle a group of rowdy, drunk men, and he'd witnessed her doing so on many occasions, but it was still nice to know that he had her back.

Reaching the car, they climbed in and Tony started the ignition. Charlotte switched on the radio, settling back in her seat as the sound of Ed Sheeran flooded the small space. Soon, they were back on the road heading away from the quayside, and up towards the headquarters on the perimeter of the city, where Rick Donovan was hopefully waiting to break his silence.

# Chapter 17

Will and I head back along the promenade, taking the same route as I had used to get to the museum. He shivers and pulls up the hood of his windbreaker, before lowering his chin into his zipped-up collar and bowing his head to the ground. It's dark now, and the temperature has plunged, largely due to the clear sky. Pitch black above us, its endless blanket is studded with a thousand stars. The streets of Morteford are now entirely deserted and a thin layer of frost is beginning to emerge, shimmering like glitter under the white glow of street lamps lining the waterfront promenade.

Will continues to chat and I listen intently as we continue the short walk back to my cottage. He tells me a little about Morteford's history, which is intriguing, as I had guessed it would be. We pause only briefly when Will stops to point out the small local docks in the distance, and his eyes light up as he tells me about his dad's boat that is moored there. It's clear to me that his father means the world to him and, when he continues to tell me more about the state of his health, it's easy to see why.

As we get closer to the cottage I begin to feel a little shaky and pick up my pace. I start to feel lightheaded as soon as we reach the corner of where the cottage is based, and find myself wondering if coming here really was a good idea after all. Maybe, despite thinking I was fine following the accident, I wasn't back to normal yet and, perhaps, I should have listened to Luke and Dad and spent more time recuperating at home.

"Are you alright, Megan?" asks Will, as we finally reach the cottage door.

"Yes, I'm OK I think, just feeling a little queasy." I clutch my stomach.

"You look very pale," he replies, and even though he's trying to hide it, I detect a concerned tone.

"I probably just need something to eat and a good night's sleep."

Will smiles.

"Well, look after yourself, Megan – it was nice chatting to you today." He starts to move away.

"Yes, you too Will." I turn away from him, retrieve the key from my pocket and, as I move towards the door, my vision blurs and my head starts to swim. Before I know it, I hit the ground. Will is instantly at my side, lifting me from the cold pavement and towards the door, as I pass out.

***

A soothing warmth hits my face as I wake up. It takes a few moments to realize that I'm lying on the sofa in the living room, and Will is on a chair next to me.

"Hi there," he leans forward and rests his hands on his knees.

"I'm so sorry Will, I don't know what happened." I exclaim, as I sit up, too quickly.

"Hey, take it easy, you blacked out, that's all," replies Will, calmly.

"For how long?"

"Only a few minutes. I hope you don't mind me bringing you inside – you had the key in your hand."

"No, not at all." I glance at the fire in front of me, crackling as it slowly builds and increases the diminished light in the room.

"It was freezing in here, so I thought I'd light it for you," offers Will, following my line of vision.

I nod back, gratefully. "Thank you!"

"Do you want me to call a doctor?" Will rises to his feet and pulls his mobile from his pocket.

"No, honestly, I'm fine. I'm prone to these blackouts – I've been having them since…"
I hesitate before continuing, "…since my husband passed away."

"Oh, I'm so sorry." Will looks down at the floor uncomfortably, "I didn't know."

"Don't worry, why would you?"

"When was it?"

"14 months ago." Tears threaten to form, but I force them away, like I always do when I tell anyone about Johnny's death. "He drowned whilst trying to save his sister, Eva, the friend I'm here with."

Will doesn't say anything, just nods slightly in response.

"Anyway, like I say, I'm used to them. They sometimes happen if I haven't had much to eat actually."

I stand up and compose myself.

"Would you like a drink or anything?" I ask. I shake off the dizziness and head towards the kitchen in search of a distraction.

"Yes please, if that's OK – I've texted Elliott to tell him I'll see him tomorrow."

"Oh, I'm sorry Will! You have plans tonight, don't you?" I pop my head back round the door.

"Not now I don't," he snaps his phone case shut, and smiles. I smile in return.

"We have tea, coffee, beer…" I shout as I move into the small kitchen and open the fridge door.

"A beer please!" shouts Will from the living room. "It is Saturday night after all!"

I return with a bottle in one hand, and a glass of red wine in the other. It's probably not the most sensible thing to have after what's just happened, but I need to calm my nervousness, not only regarding Detective Morgan being back in touch, but also about having a drink with a stranger in my cottage!

"Eva brought *some* supplies with us," I laugh, "there's absolutely no food in the fridge, but enough alcohol to sink a ship."

Will chuckles, "Girl after my own heart then!"

"Actually, I thought Eva would be back by now," I say, glancing at my watch.

"I think I heard your phone alert while you were unconscious," replies Will, nodding to my handbag resting on the coffee table. He takes a sip from the bottle.

I place my wine down, retrieve the phone from my bag, and read out a text message from Eva.

"Going better than I thought so I might be back a *little* later tonight. Really sorry Meg! I'll make it up to you tomorrow, E xoxo."

"Oh, well done Jack!" replies Will, raising his bottle in a silent toast.

I smile and quickly respond, telling her to relax and enjoy herself. Eva's been through a terrible time too. Not only has she lost her twin brother, who she adored, but she has to deal with the constant guilt that Johnny's death was her fault and, no matter how many times people tell her that it was nothing more than a tragic accident, I doubt that she will ever be able to forgive herself.

As my closest friend, she deserves to start enjoying herself again, and rebuild her life. As do I.

"How are you feeling now?" asks Will, taking another sip from his bottle.

"Much better, thanks." I drag my fingers through my windswept hair and rub my eyes. *God, I must look a sight.*

"You look great!" says Will sheepishly, as if reading my mind.

Something about him makes me feel at ease and, after an initial, slightly awkward introduction this morning, I now see that he is a decent guy who I can genuinely say I've enjoyed spending time with.

*** 

We spend the next couple of hours just chatting. I order a pizza from the neighbouring town and, as we tuck in, we laugh and talk about ourselves, like we've been friends for years. At 10.30 pm, Will places his fifth empty bottle on the floor and gets to his feet.

"Well I'd better get going, before your friend gets back," he says, reaching for his jacket.

"Yes. It was really nice chatting with you, Will." I say cheerily, standing to face him. I suddenly feel the happiest I can remember in a very long time, and I can't decide if it's a result of spending time with Will, or the almost-empty bottle of wine, which sits on the floor.

"Thank you, again, for rescuing me, and for helping me out earlier, too."

I reach up to give him a peck on the cheek and, as I pull away, he rests his hand on my hip and our eyes meet. Heat from the open fire blazes against my skin, his eyes are flecked orange from the open flames and then, suddenly, he kisses me. It's just a peck at first, but then develops and, although I can't deny that it feels incredible, it also somehow feels wrong. I haven't been this close to a man since I lost Johnny, and I instantly feel guilty, so pull away to create a space between us.

"Goodnight, Will."

He takes the hint and heads to the front door, looking as guilt-ridden as I feel.

"Goodnight, Megan. Look after yourself."

I hear the door close, but less than a minute later, Eva bursts through it.

"Who was that man I just saw leaving?" she questions, her eyes wide as she races to the window and watches Will disappear round the corner of the street. She slowly turns and stares back at me, with a huge, shocked smile on her face. "Oh Meg…. is that who I think it is?"

"Who?" I ask, smiling innocently. My heart's still racing from the kiss, and my cheeks are on fire.

Eva raises her eyebrows, "You know who – Will Travers!"

"Yes! I bumped into him this afternoon and then had one of my funny turns – he helped me…again," I reply, as casually as I can. Eva still has a huge grin on her face. It's clear that she wants more detail, but soon realizes that I don't want to divulge, so she swiftly changes the subject to her afternoon spent with Jack. I settle back on the sofa and try to absorb what she's telling me, fighting the urge to race past her, out the door and after Will.

Later, when I'm lying in bed, my mind is racing and won't let me rest. I think about Will, and Johnny. As always, I curl up on the right side of the bed and allow myself the belief that there is a heavy arm, reassuringly draped over me. However, tonight, I question whose touch I want to feel.

An hour or so later, exhaustion takes over and I finally drift off to sleep, sinking into the same dream I have had almost every night for the past week, where I am being rescued from a burning car by a gorgeous stranger.

# Chapter 18

As Eva drops me home, Luke is coming out and he takes the heavy case from me. I search my bag for my keys as he misses catching the open door in time, and it slams shut behind him.

"Did you and Eva have a good time?" he asks, dropping the case in the hallway as I finally open the door. It crashes on its side on the marble floor.

"Yeah, it was good," I reply, convincingly.

In reality, I hadn't seen very much of Eva. This morning, although she'd promised we would spend it together, she had met up again with the elusive Jack Dalton and, as a result, I'd spent the morning watching television, hiding from the possibility of bumping into Will again.

"Are you coming in for a cuppa Luke?"

"No thanks. I've got to get home and changed as I've got footie practice. I just thought I'd pop in and feed Tilly on my way there, as I wasn't sure what time you were getting back."

"Thanks for looking after her for a couple of days, Luke. I appreciate it."

"No probs! You got anything planned for the rest of today?"

"Not really," I reply, glancing up at the cloudless blue sky. "Think I'll go for a walk actually."

"OK, well look after yourself, sis." Luke pecks me on the cheek. "I'll see you tomorrow for dinner at Dad's."

"Yes, you too. See you then."

I wave as he drives away. There was nothing more that our mum loved to see than us all sitting round the dinner table, tucking into her weekly roast and, since she died, it's a regular tradition we make sure we keep.

\*\*\*

It's getting colder by the time I get to the cemetery and, although I'm aware that I should really call DCI Morgan as I'd promised, for some reason I can't do it yet. Instead, I've spent the last hour walking and as always when I go for a stroll these days, I've ended up at the cemetery, standing before Johnny's memorial plaque.

Crouching down to reach his stone, I brush away the crispy, orange leaves that have fallen from the oak tree overhead and I pull my coat sleeve over my hand to polish the dried soil from its surface. Even though either myself, Eva or Johnny's parents visit every week to tend to it, it's difficult to keep on top of it during the winter months.

A noise close by breaks the silence of the deserted cemetery and makes me jump. It's then that I notice a large black crow perched on a gravestone a few rows down. It cocks its head as if questioning why I'm there, before flying off into the trees. Holding my hand against the cold marble, I trace Johnny's name, and then I remove my wedding ring and trace the same initials engraved inside.

As always, I think of Johnny – trying to recapture the memories of the early years in our relationship, when we were both young, carefree and totally besotted. However, I am now also compelled to relive the memories of closer to the time of his death, when we were overworked, stressed and barely had time for one another.

Unfortunately, Johnny and I had drifted apart during the last couple of years leading to his death. We hardly saw each other and, when we did, we ended up arguing. I'd like to believe that what others saw from outside our marriage, was still true. In reality though, and if I'm honest with myself, our marriage was more than halfway to being over.

Johnny and I loved each other, we always had, but sometimes love alone isn't enough. Maybe the crow was right!

A cracking sound nearby drags me from my memories and back to my senses. Standing up, I brush the dried dirt from my jeans and look around. In the dwindling twilight of the extensive cemetery grounds, it's hard to see, but I can clearly make out a silhouette standing by a tree, not too far away.

Slowly, I begin to make my way over and although I can't make out who they are, I can tell that their attention is focused on me. They realize I've seen them and begin to quickly walk away. I follow, keeping my sights set on the stalker and, quickening my pace, I begin to jog. They do the same and by the time I get to the tree, they've gone. Vanished. I wonder who it is, and, actually, if there was anyone there at all. Maybe it was Johnny's ghost and my mind playing tricks, like it used to in the weeks after Johnny first died when I would see him in the house all the time – standing in the corner of the bedroom studying me, or sitting on the bottom of the bed watching me sleep. Sometimes I'd see him lying in the empty bathtub before I switched on the bathroom light, or waiting for me at the top of the stairs. The image seemed so real; his skin pale and bruised, his eyes empty and lifeless. He was always wearing the same clothes, dressed head to toe in white; the same outfit he'd worn the last time I saw him and said goodbye, when he left for the airport with Eva. There was no emotion then – his unknowingly final kiss loveless and cold.

In the early days of losing him, when I saw these visions, I would scream, close my eyes, and, on opening them again, he would be gone. I soon learned that the visions were nothing more than grief, coupled with an overactive imagination; something I've been burdened with since I was a small child.

Although I still occasionally see Johnny, I'm now aware that it's just my mind playing tricks, and I'm no longer scared by it.

Walking back to the cemetery exit, I see a car enter through the iron gates ahead and it makes its way down the road towards me. It's pretty dark now, and the headlights blind me at first, once again making me think about the accident. I'm suddenly aware that I'm alone, in a deserted cemetery, and how careless it is of me not to contact the police when I arrived home. I suddenly begin to panic!

The car continues towards me and I look around for another path I can take, but the gate I'm heading towards is the only one open. I freeze, and as the car pulls over, the driver's window is wound down. At that point relief rushes through me.

"Meg! I didn't know you were coming here today?" Eva shuffles over from the driver's side and pops open the passenger door for me to climb in.

"Neither did I really," I reply, as I sit down. "I just fancied some fresh air after you dropped me off." I take off my gloves and rub my hands in front of the warming heaters. I didn't tell Eva about the call from Morgan yesterday, and I don't mention the police wanting to see me; I have no intention of worrying her unnecessarily.

"Hi, Aunty Meg!" A little voice emerges from the darkness in the back of the car and I turn to see Maisie, smiling back at me, a toy rabbit in one hand and a packet of crisps in the other.

"We've just been to see mum and dad," says Eva, pulling away from the cemetery gates in the direction that I had just walked. "I thought I'd pop here before we head home – I've brought some flowers to lay down, for Johnny." She points to a small and pretty winter bouquet, resting on the back seat next to Maisie. "I've been thinking about him a lot since we went to Morteford; memories of us as kids, you know?"

I nod thoughtfully. "Yes, I understand."

Eva pulls up, close to Johnny's stone, and opens her door.

"I'll be 2 minutes and then I'll give you a lift home. It's too cold for you to be roaming the streets."

"Thanks, Eva," I reply, gratefully.

"How are you then gorgeous?" I ask Maisie, as I watch Eva wander down the narrow footpath towards the stone. I turn in my seat to get a clear view of my niece. It's only a few weeks since I last saw her, but I'm sure she has grown in that time. She's wearing a pink polka-dot coat; her naturally blonde hair hanging down to her waist, and her striking blue eyes peer back at me in the faintly lit car. She looks more and more like Eva as she gets older, and, because Eva and Johnny were so alike, it's hard not to visualize him in Maisie too.

"I'm fine, thank you, Auntie Meg. Are you?" I smile at her manners – polite as always – not something you could say about many 6-year-olds.

"Oh I'm great, thanks!"

"Would you like one?" Maisie leans towards me and offers her packet of crisps.

"Oh, yes please!" I reach forward and take one; it's shaped like an animal of some sort, I can't decide which one.

"You can have another if you want?"

I pop the crisp into my mouth, filling it with flavour, and it's only then that I realize I haven't eaten anything today. My stomach grumbles in discontentment.

"No, you're OK sweetheart – you go ahead and finish them." Maisie smiles, and continues to munch on her snack.

"What's Mummy doing?" Maisie queries, once she's finished eating; placing her head against the back-seat window to watch Eva.

"She's visiting Uncle Johnny." I give my niece a reassuring glance in the rearview mirror.

Maisie nods, understanding. "Is Uncle Johnny in heaven now?"

"Yes, darling. He is."

"Is he an angel?"

I can't help but smile at Maisie's question before I answer her.

"Yes, I'm sure he is."

At Maisie's young age, it was difficult to explain, when he died, as she loved him very much, but all things considered, she has taken his death extremely well. It's true that he was a loving, caring and generous man towards his niece, and someone who Maisie looked up to, but he was far from an angel!

I watch as Eva reaches Johnny's grave and kneels in front of it, just as I had done earlier. She mutters a few silent words and places the flowers down, putting her fingers to her lips and kissing them before placing her hand gently on her brother's name; after a few minutes, she makes her way back to the car.

Climbing in, she starts the ignition and wipes a tear from her eye.

"Right," she smiles sadly, "let's get you home."

\*\*\*

It's gone 6 pm by the time I'm home and, when the doorbell rings, I'm not surprised to see who's there as I've prepared myself for whatever they have to say.

"Hi Megan. Is it OK if we come in?" DI Taylor asks, before the door's even fully open. She's already halfway through it when I respond, and my heart beats quickly. I once again think how irresponsible I've been not to call them to tell them I was home before now.

"Yes, I'm so sorry! I know I was supposed to call, but I only got back from Morteford half an hour ago," I say, untruthfully. Morgan glares at me, and I know immediately that he thinks I'm lying. In hindsight, I've probably done myself no favours in avoiding them.

"Don't worry about it Megan. We were passing by and thought we'd check you were here," says DCI Morgan, as he follows Taylor into the living room.

"We have some news about the crash, Megan," announces DI Taylor, choosing to sit in the same place on the sofa as she did last time. She doesn't look quite as pristine as she did previously; her long, blonde hair is pulled back into a grip at the nape of her neck and her complexion is pale, with dark circles shadowing her eyes.

"Really?" I sit down opposite them. "Have you caught the kids who were driving the car?"

"We've caught the owner of the car, but it wasn't kids. Do you remember me asking you if the name Rick Donovan meant anything to you?"

"Yes."

"Well, we believe he was the man behind the wheel of that car."

I'm more confused than ever.

"Erm, OK," is all I manage to say.

DCI Morgan continues.

"We still haven't found that car, but we have discovered some CCTV footage from a nearby garage, which captured a car as it left the area. It was around the time the incident occurred, and it fits the description that you gave to the police officers when they visited you in hospital."

I nod.

"Rick Donovan is a well-known criminal, Megan. He's been on our radar for many years and was released from prison almost 2 years ago. Since then, he's been on his best behaviour, but he's an extremely clever man and has, up until now, always been one step ahead of us. This time it appears he was not so lucky."

The room starts to swim and I grab the side of the sofa, understanding what Morgan is sensitively trying to tell me and forcing back another black-out episode.

"You're telling me that this man tried to kill me?"

"We believe so Megan. Yes."

"But, why?"

"That's what we're trying to find out. He's not talking much yet, but we believe we will get to him soon."

I take a deep breath. "I just don't understand. Why would anyone purposely want to run me off the road?"

"As we said, we don't know…yet." DI Taylor pulls a file from her bag and removes a photo.

"Do you recognize this man, Megan?"

I study the photo, more commonly known as a mug shot. The man staring back looks fairly ordinary; late 50s/early 60s, with an unshaven, grey stubbly face, dark, steely-grey eyes and a full head of silver hair. It's immediately apparent to me that I've never seen this man before in my life.

"No, I've definitely never seen him before," I say with certainty, pushing the photo back across the coffee table in Taylor's direction.

"Are you sure?" she asks, sliding the photo back to me.

"Yes, I'm *absolutely* sure!" I repeat, impatiently. I don't like being kept in the dark and in this case I feel it's pitch black!

"Any silly feuds with anyone, petty arguments?"

"No!"

Morgan nods, "do you know of anyone at all you feel would want to harm you in any way?"

"No. Most definitely not!" I can't help but feel insulted by Morgan's ridiculous questions.

He nods and looks at Taylor, who is staring at me, searching my face for answers. Her bright green eyes are cold and I wonder if she thinks I'm lying to them.

"Alright," she says abruptly, and then adds "we'll be in touch if anything new comes up."

I stare back at her dumbfounded. *They have just told me that someone purposely tried to kill me, and they are just going to leave…?*

Taylor finally stands, prompting Morgan to rise too, and they both move towards the door. Morgan obviously notices a look of trepidation cross my face and he slows his pace before reaching the hall.

"You're not in any danger now, Megan. We have Donovan safely in custody, which is where he will stay until we can get to the bottom of this."

I manage a smile, before seeing them out.

"Please call us straightaway if there's anything at all you need," Morgan smiles back, and for the first time since we met, I notice a softness to him that I'd not detected before.

"Thank you," I reply.

Then they are gone and once again, I am alone.

# Chapter 19

Will was sitting at his usual table in the Anchor. He'd only been there an hour, had already downed four pints, and had no intention of stopping anytime soon. He made his way to the bar; as normal for a Sunday, it was heaving.

"Can I get another Carling, please Mike?" he pushed his way to the front where Mike was standing, and placed his empty glass on the bar. He hadn't seen Mike yet and, up until now, had been served by Lisa, Mike's daughter, and one of Elliott's many ex-girlfriends.

"Yes, no problem, Will. How's things?"

"Fine, thanks." Will tried to hide the annoyance in his voice and pretend that things were as they always were. Inside, he was raging and could feel himself reaching boiling point as the hours rolled on.

"Oh, I forgot to tell you!" Mike finished pulling the pint and levelled the head on it. "There was a young lady looking for you in here, on Friday night."

"Yeah, I know."

"Did she manage to track you down?"

"She did, yes."

Mike raised his eyebrows, "There are worse problems than having a pretty girl desperate to find you!" Will managed a smile through gritted teeth and, taking his pint, returned to his window seat.

Half an hour later, Elliott made his way to the table.

"Sorry I'm late mate! Had to pop over and check on the guys at the apartment to see how they're getting on. They called me an hour ago to tell me they're having problems with the electrics…again." Elliott shrugged off his coat. His cheeks were rosy from the cold and he looked frozen.

Will nodded, finding it difficult to look his old friend in the eye, and even harder to make general chit-chat. Elliott left him to get a drink, returning with a bottle of cider, and he pulled up the stool opposite. Will chose that moment to look Elliott in the eye, and he wondered how long it would take for him to tell Will what he already knew.

"So, I suppose you want me to tell you exactly what happened yesterday?" asked Elliott, gingerly. It was obvious that he'd picked up on Will's anger.

Will felt it bubbling inside him. He had planned on letting Elliott tell him his side of the story – he deserved a chance to explain, but fury got the better of him and he couldn't hold it in any longer.

"What the hell were you thinking, Elliott?" he snapped, before Elliott could speak. He kept his voice low, although he wanted nothing more than to scream in his face. He was well aware of the fact that there were ears everywhere, and it didn't take long for this small village to start gossiping if peace in the community was disturbed. Even a childish, drunken squabble, if not kept under wraps, was pretty much front-page news the following morning.

Elliott looked scolded, like a small child caught eating sweets before meal time.

"Erm, I'm not sure what you mean Will," he replied, unable to meet Will's eyes.

"One favour! I asked you for *one favour* as my best mate and you couldn't even get that right!"

"Actually, I did what you asked," Elliott responded impatiently.

Will laughed sarcastically, "yeah, plus a few additional extras thrown in for good measure!"

"What do you mean by that?"

"I asked you to go and meet Megan at the office, take the key back, and accept her gratitude – that was it!"

"Yeah, which I did."

"Then you accidentally bumped into her again, somehow, and ended up back at her cottage?"

Elliott lowered his head again.

"What if anyone had seen you, Elliott?"

"Well, they didn't! I did what you asked of me Will, I pretended to be you!"

"And what part of 'pretending to be me' involved kissing her?"

Elliott was clearly taken aback. "You saw?"

"Yes, Elliott, I saw."

"How?"

"I was on my way home and thought I'd peek in at the cottage window to check she was OK. I didn't expect to see you slobbering all over her!"

"It wasn't like that," Elliott muttered, reaching for his bottle and taking a hefty swig before slamming it back down on the table.

"It wasn't like what?" asked Will.

"I did what you asked and pretended to be you at the office. I didn't know I was going to bump into her at the museum, and I certainly didn't plan it that way. I had just popped in for a coffee, on the way back from the apartment, so I couldn't exactly ignore her, could I?"

"Yes, yes, Elliott you could."

Elliott took another long swig and shook his head angrily at his friend.

"Does she know about me?" asked Will.

"No! I pretended to be you all night."

"Oh great, this just gets better."

"Megan is amazing, Will. *Really* amazing."

Will looked down at his feet, his temper subsiding a little. "Yes, I don't doubt that."

"I'm sorry! There was just something about her...I really like her Will."

"You can't see her again!" Will's tone was lowered again and he now felt a little guilty for confronting Elliott the way he had.

"Yes, I'm aware of that, but you're going to have to come clean with her at some point you know. It's not fair to string her along."

Aggravated, Will ignored Elliott and got up from his seat. Pulling his wallet from his pocket, he turned to get another drink.

"She deserves to know the truth Will."

Will stopped dead in his tracks, his back to Elliott who continued. "You have to tell Megan that it was you who rescued her that night, and she needs to know who you really are."

# Chapter 20

"Are you alright, pet?" My dad takes away my plate – still filled with a barely touched roast dinner.

"Yes, thanks Dad, I'm fine."

"But you've barely touched your dinner." My dad looks concerned.

"I know, I'm just not hungry. Think I might be coming down with a bug or something."

My dad nods, seeming to accept my lies, and he continues to clear the table. I rise to help him, but he orders me to sit back down and take it easy.

"You back at work tomorrow?" asks Luke, who has already plonked himself on the sofa and is lying stretched out in front of the TV.

"Yeah."

"You sure you're ready?" he asks and, taking his eyes off the TV he looks behind to where I'm still sitting at the table.

"It's as good a time as any I suppose," I reply.

In all honesty, up until yesterday, I was ready to put my suit back on and return to work. However, after the visit from DCI Morgan and DI Taylor, and the news they had relayed, I'm now not sure I'm in the right frame of mind. The image of Rick Donovan keeps dominating my thoughts and, after a terrible, sleepless night, still nothing makes sense. At least I know

Donovan is in police custody, and I trust that Morgan and Taylor will do their job and find out what is going on.

I pick up the bowls from the table and head into the kitchen where my dad is busy washing up. I pull a clean tea towel from the warm radiator and begin to dry.

"I told you to sit down, Meg. I can manage."

"Don't be daft, Dad – a few dishes aren't going to kill me!" My dad smiles and shakes his head, knowing that there's no point in arguing. Although he and Luke would like to believe otherwise, ever since mum died I have been the boss in this family and they know when to admit defeat.

"So, you enjoyed your weekend away with Eva then?" asks my dad, as he hands me a glass and starts on the pans. An image of Will pops into my head and I instinctively put my hand to my lips.

"Yeah, it was pretty good."

"Where did you say you went?" he asks.

"I'm not sure if I did, but we went to a little fishing village that Eva and Johnny used to visit with their mum and dad, when they were kids. It's called Morteford."

Without looking up from the sinkful of soapy water in front of him, my dad replies,

"Oh, Morteford, yes, I know it well."

"Really? You've been there before?"

"Oh yes. I worked just along the coast from there, back in the day, at a shipbuilders. It was when I moved back to the North East, just before your mother and I met."

"Really? I didn't know that." I'm not really surprised that my dad had worked near Morteford as he'd been in the shipbuilding trade for years and had been based on the Tyne for the vast majority of the time he and mum were married. Before then, his job had taken him all over the country.

"Yep, worked there for a couple of years, then got a contract closer to home so I moved back here permanently. Thank God I did because that's when I met your Mam."

Dad looks out of the kitchen window at the weak autumn sun filtering through, clearly reminiscing his younger days.

"It's a beautiful place," he adds, his attention returned. "Although it might have changed now; I haven't been back since I worked there and that would have been, hmm, 35 years ago now."

"Yes," I nod, "it's still a very pretty place.

My dad continues to reminisce.

"I had a little flat, which overlooked the water."

"Very nice – I could think of worse places to work."

"Aye love, it was canny. Shared it with my mate, Bob Simmonds, who I worked with at the time. You remember old Bobby Simmonds, don't you?"

"Yes, Dad, I remember him well. He was a lovely man."

"Aye, he was, you don't get many like him anymore. Salt of the earth. I met a lovely girl there too, Jenny May she was called."

"Ooh, get you Casanova." I slap my dad playfully with the end of the damp tea towel, and smile. It's not very often that he talks about his life before mum. I assume it's because she had been such a massive part of his life since. They would have been married almost 31 years had she still been alive, and she was, and always will be, the love of his life. It was the sort of

131

love I envied as a child, pure and unconditional, and I hoped one day to find that.

Finishing the dishes, we join Luke in the living room. Dad falls asleep on his recliner like he does every week, while Luke and I sit in front of the TV, muttering the occasional word to each other. Today though Luke is a lot chattier than he usually is, which is a pleasant surprise. He asks me all about my trip to Morteford and I tell him how pretty the place is and what a great time Eva and I had. Just as I have done with Dad, I sugarcoat everything and don't mention my real reason for being there because, like Dad, I don't want Luke to worry. They've both been through too much to add any more worries.

Half an hour later, I'm standing in the kitchen, tucking into a packet of digestives while waiting for the kettle to boil, when something suddenly hits me. Rushing through to the living room, I tell Luke that I have to go – making a work-related excuse – and I step out of Dad's house, into the cold autumn air, to make my way home.

# Chapter 21

The following day I don't have time to contemplate my nervousness about driving. My brain is too occupied by other matters as I think I've discovered the truth, and now I have to get to Morteford as soon as I can. I have no idea why it's taken me so long to figure it out.

There are no flights until later this evening, and the train will end up taking longer than it would to drive, so I've hired a car and left, early morning, without telling anyone where I was going. I've called my boss and told him I need another few days off sick. As always, he totally understands and tells me that he needs me fighting fit when I do return, as we have a massive contract coming our way. Normally, this type of news would be at the forefront of my mind and I'd be playing with ideas in my head; already planning my pitch. Today, I have more important things to think about.

The fury has fuelled me to get there, and because my mind has been kept so busy, the trip passes pretty quickly. It's only now, as I approach the bend that leads me into the neighbouring town, that I'm starting to have doubts again.

I'd spent the best part of last night searching the internet for a 'William Travers', located in Morteford. It seems that he must be one of a small minority who doesn't dabble in the delights of social media and, although I managed to find some written information about his business, through the A.W.E.

company homepage, other than his date of birth, and the fact that he has won quite a few awards in the field, it told me little more than I already knew. In the end, I found no hard evidence to back my suspicion of who Will Travers really is, but my gut feeling is proof enough for me.

I continue the drive towards Morteford, my brain bursting with questions. Again, when I see the road sign which reads 'Morteford – 2 miles', I feel more doubts creeping in.

*Could I be jumping to conclusions?* I am the first to acknowledge my downfalls, and admit that, diving in, head first, without thinking things through, has always been one of them. I think of the conversations I had with Will while I was in Morteford, how he behaved at our first meeting, and also that I somehow knew he was lying when he said he was 'just passing' on the night of the accident. *Had he been following me? Did he not come to the hospital because he feared he would be found out, or was all this just a crazy coincidence?*

I pull up outside the apartment at the top of the hill leading into Morteford. It's gone lunchtime now and, as Will had mentioned he normally came here first thing in the morning before heading to the office, I really hoped he would still be here. I don't relish the thought of getting the ferry over to Fadstow on such a cold day.

I ring the bell five times before the same woman who Eva and I had spoken to when we were here last, opens it. She eyes me just as suspiciously as she had 5 days ago.

"Can I help you?"

"I'm looking for Will Travers!" I say, without pleasantries. I was too nice to her last time and this woman is clearly just a nasty cow. Well, two can play that game.

"You were here the other night looking for him. Who are you?" the woman asks rudely.

"None of your business! Is he here?"

The woman steps to one side, allowing me to push past her.

"Apartment three," she shouts, defeated, as I make my way along a lengthy corridor.

The door to apartment three is partially open when I reach it, and it creaks on its hinges as I swing it open to reveal an empty room.

"Hello?"

No response apart from my own voice echoing around the massive space. Dust cloths cover the wooden floors; ladders are set up in the corner, and electric wires hang from the walls and ceiling. A huge old fireplace is covered over with plastic sheeting; the beautiful decorative tiles underneath clearly visible, and halfway through being painstakingly restored to their former glory. Dust particles dance in the weak light, highlighted by two huge arched windows looking out over the golden shore of the estuary, a clear view to Fadstow in the near distance. Although a mess now, there is no denying that the place has immeasurable potential.

The door bangs shut behind me as an icy draught floods the musty air of the apartment, causing me to shiver.

"Hi, is anybody here?" I ask, nervously.

I make my way to the opposite side of the room, my trainers squeaking on the unprotected parts of old parquet flooring.

"Hello?" I repeat.

I reach another door and call out again, but there's no answer; this place is empty. I'm just about to leave, planning my trip over to Will's office in Fadstow, when a deep recognizable voice answers.

"Hi, I'm sorry, I was just—" Will stops dead in his tracks when he sees me, his mouth visibly dropping open as he comes through the main door of the apartment.

"Megan, hi… erm, what are you doing here?"

Rage erupts as I race across the room and shove him as hard as I can in the chest. I don't know where the strength comes from, but it seems that all of my pent-up emotions since finding out what I am now 99% sure is the truth, have come out in one fell swoop. Caught off guard, Will loses his balance and falls backwards into a pile of cardboard boxes.

"You bastard!"

Will struggles to get up from the boxes.

"What the hell?"

"You told me that your dad's old fishing boat in the harbour was named 'Jenny May', after your mum. The boat he used before he got sick."

Will looks at me blankly, so I continue.

"Jennifer May is the name of the woman my dad had a relationship with, and she lived in the same village. You were born almost 8 months after he left Morteford and returned to Newcastle, just before he and my mother met!"

136

Will remains silent.

"Then, you show up on a deserted country bridge that hardly anyone uses, at just the right time to save me. You don't come to the hospital, and you don't give a name because you didn't want anyone finding out who you really are. Now, tell me Will, is all this just a huge coincidence?"

Will eventually manages to free himself from the boxes and stands to look at me.

"It's not what you think, Megan."

"And what am I thinking?" I shove him again, but this time he's prepared and doesn't budge an inch.

"You're my half-brother, aren't you? You were watching me that night. It's the only possible way you would have seen the car at the bottom of the ravine and that's why you were so funny with me the day I came to see you at the office. You were worried you'd been rumbled!"

Will stays silent – he doesn't need words. The look on his face says it all; he's my brother!

"Tell me the bloody truth Will, it's the least I deserve." My voice sounds calm, but I feel anything but. I've always hated liars; I find men who lie are the weakest of their kind. My husband was no exception.

I think of Will kissing me back in the cottage, and of the thoughts I've had about him since I left Morteford. I clench my stomach and bend forward, feeling physically sick.

When I stand up straight again, Will has moved so that he is directly in front of me, but his focus is set on something over my shoulder at the other side of the room.

"No, I'm not your brother," answers Will quietly, running his hands through his hair, which is full of white dust.

I step back from him; my trainers once again squeaking on the flooring. It's then that I hear another voice behind me.

"He's not your brother, Megan, but I am!"

# Chapter 22

Charlotte reached forward and paused the recorder on the table. Standing up slowly, she made sure that she kept her glare fixed on Donovan and, although his grey eyes bore into hers, his expression remained vacant. She forcibly tore away her stare. She really needed to take a break, and Joe Emery nodded at her silently as she made to leave. No words were even needed – it was abundantly clear that she had to get out of this room and away from Donovan, before she did something she would undoubtedly later regret.

Emery joined her in the corridor, "Go and get yourself a coffee and take a break Taylor, you look like you need it," he said softly.

"Thank you, sir," she replied, gratefully.

In the short time that Charlotte had been in Newcastle she had grown fond of Detective Superintendent Emery, not just because of all the positive things she'd heard about him from Tony, but because he was clearly a decent bloke and excellent at his job. Even though he refused to admit it, Charlotte was sure he could see how similar she was to him.

Unfortunately Donovan was clever! He knew exactly how to press her buttons and had successfully riled her within the first few minutes of the interview, just as he had done with Tony when Emery called them in last night.

After years with no visual contact, Donovan had been face to face with the man who put him behind bars – DCI Tony Morgan. Normally refusing to show any weakness, Donovan's expression had visibly dropped when he saw Tony enter the interview room, although seconds later a fake smile appeared before his first words to him in almost a decade.

"Oh hello–again–DCI Morgan, long time no see eh? Tell me, how is your lovely wife, Olivia, doing, and the kids?"

To anybody who didn't know Donovan's capabilities, this would have been nothing more than a friendly greeting. However, in this case it was a personal message to Tony. Donovan had clearly kept tabs on him over the years, and used their reunion to pose an indirect threat.

Charlotte could have sworn that Tony was going to put Donovan in an early grave as he lunged across the table that separated the two men, and she watched, with interest, as Emery calmly stepped in and dismissed Tony from the interview.

Never before had she seen so much fury and hatred in Tony's eyes. His untypically emotional reaction to Donovan's successful attempt to rile him had given her a small glimpse into a side of Tony Morgan she had not previously witnessed. She was actually quite impressed! It only confirmed to her what she had known from the first moment she met him; how genuine a man Tony was, and how much he cared for his family.

Charlotte quickly left the interview room, heading along the corridor and up a single flight of steps, her small heels clicking on the polished linoleum floor. Stopping at the end of the corridor, she smoothed her hair over her shoulders and composed herself. She wanted to appear calm when she saw Tony, even though Donovan made her feel the exact opposite.

She didn't bother to knock on his door before she entered. When it was only the two of them in the office, they knew each other well enough to bypass the usual politeness.

Turning on his chair to face her, Tony looked as exhausted as she felt.

"How you doing?" he asked, wearily.

Charlotte wrinkled her nose.

"Better than me last night I hope?" Tony asked, concentrating on her as he ran his hand through his rapidly greying dark hair.

She wanted to pretend that things were OK, for no other reason than to keep Tony's morale positive. She couldn't pinpoint exactly what it was about Donovan's actions, but Tony's energy had appeared to be bled dry.

"Not really! I'm bloody fed up to be honest – Donovan's going on like he's a sodding angel!" As always, her thoughts were revealed before she had chance to choose the appropriate words.

Tony sighed. "To be fair on him, he hasn't set a foot wrong since he got out of prison last...until this happened, anyway."

It was evident that Tony losing his temper yesterday was a blip, and he was now back to being the logical and dexterous DCI that she knew and admired.

"Yeah, that we know of." Charlotte reached past Tony into the top drawer of his desk and pulled out an unopened Maltesers share bag. Biting off the corner, she poured a quarter of the contents into her hand, before returning the packet to the drawer and throwing herself onto a chair.

No matter where they were based, Tony would always have a drawer (or a glove compartment), offering sweets and chocolate. Considering they'd only been back here for a few days, he already had this one impressively well stocked and it was almost as good as the drawer back at home. On days like this, when allowing enough time for an actual lunch break was nothing but a fantasy, the drawer always offered a well-needed sugar boost to keep energy levels functional.

"Good to see the case isn't affecting your appetite!" Tony smiled, his mood lifting.

Charlotte slumped further down into her seat, ignoring his sarcasm. Normally she would bite back with a lighthearted retort, but today she just wasn't in the mood. Maybe Donovan had got to her too.

She couldn't believe how calm Tony seemed now, and concluded that some reflective time overnight had helped. He was back to his usual professional manner, someone who knew the rule book inside out and rarely went against it.

"Do you think Donovan's telling us the truth, Tony?"

"What, that his car was stolen the night of Megan's accident? Yeah, I actually think he could be."

"Then why didn't he just tell us that from the start, why string us along?"

"He would have been waiting for advice from his lawyer. He knows better than to talk to us without legal aid, plus, he knows full well that it wouldn't take much for him to end up back behind bars."

Charlotte popped the chocolate into her mouth, but continued to talk through crunching.

"So, if it wasn't him driving that night then who the hell was it, because we know it wasn't just kids!"

Tony surveyed the busy unit through the glass door behind Charlotte.

Reaching into the sweet drawer himself, he pulled out the half-empty packet of Maltesers, tipping out a handful before answering.

"I don't know yet Taylor, but I can promise you one thing … we are sure as hell going to find out!"

# Chapter 23

I turn slowly around to see who the other voice is coming from and I'm met by what I can only describe as my brother's doppelganger.

"I'll take it from here, Elliott," he says to the man I *thought* was Will.

"What do you mean?" I ask. "Who the hell is Elliott?" My brain feels overloaded and I point to the man standing directly in front of me, who's still covered in dust from the boxes.

"You mean, he's *not* Will?!"

"No Megan, I'm Will! Elliott is my best friend and business partner. He just pretended to be me."

I look back at the man I have now been told is Elliott; the same man who, only 4 days ago, kissed me with more passion than I have ever felt. I stare at him, bewildered, and he nods to confirm that it's true.

"So, you're Will?" I spin back around and put my hand to my head. I'm normally more than capable of dealing with confusing scenarios, but this is too much for me to take in.

I take a hesitant step closer to who I now know is the 'real' Will.

"You're my…my half-brother then?" I ask. I want to look him straight in the eye, but, just like Luke, the height difference makes it impossible. I move even nearer. Close up, he doesn't look as much like Luke as I had first thought, but still, the resemblance is uncanny.

"Yes, Meg I'm your real brother!"

I look at Elliott again and I can't deny that, although shocked, I am pretty relieved!

Will seems to tap into my thoughts and chuckles slightly.

"Don't worry, he's not related to you in any way. The two of you didn't *almost* commit incest the other night!"

I can't hold back and I slap him, hard, across the face. Just like Elliott, he remains rooted to the spot. Joking or not, now is clearly not the time or place to be a smart arse!

"What the hell is going on?" I ask Will, feeling as upset and confused as the day I learnt of Johnny's death. "Were you the one who rescued me from the car then?"

Will rubs his face gingerly as my red hand imprint emerges on his clean-shaven cheek.

"Yes, yes I was."

"Why didn't *he* just explain?" I point back at Elliott who is still staring at me open mouthed.

"Because he couldn't!" His soothing tone and coolness is infuriating and only makes me feel more exasperated. I start muttering expletives under my breath.

"I'll just erm… leave you two to it," says Elliott quietly, finally breaking his silence. He begins to edge nervously towards the door.

"You stay there!" I snap, pointing a shaky finger at him. "You also owe me an explanation."

The two men glance guiltily at each other across the room, before Elliott moves to stand next to Will. Both men are roughly the same height and build, and looking at them together now, it's easy to see how I could have thought it was Elliott who rescued me on the night of the accident.

"Why couldn't you just tell me, Will?" I repeat, "I don't understand! I know my dad, understandably, had a past before he and Mum met – it's no secret!"

"Yes, but he didn't know he had another son did he?"

"No, that part he certainly doesn't know about." I admit. I take in a deep breath and attempt to calm down. It's not the existence of another brother that's making me angry, it's the deceit.

"When did you find out?" I ask. My attention focuses back on Will.

"Find out what – that my dad isn't who I thought he was? I found out a few weeks before your crash."

"How?"

"As you know, my dad, Alf, has been very ill."

"Yes, Will, Elliott… whoever the hell he is … has already told me that!" I catch Elliott's eye and, although he looks hurt, I couldn't care less.

"My mum broke down a few weeks ago and told me that the man I thought to be my father, isn't. She met Alf when she was pregnant with me, and he raised me as his own."

"So he knows that you aren't his?"

"Yes, of course, but he doesn't know that I know! If he did, it would finish him off. He has only been given a few more months to live and I can't risk him finding out."

"I see, so, why track *me* down?"

"Curiosity at first, I suppose. I was in Newcastle on business; that much is true. Mum had told me your dad's name so I'd done some research online and found out the name of the company you work for. I wanted to see where you live, so I followed you home the night you were involved in the accident."

"What about Dad and Luke – have you been spying on them too?"

"I haven't been spying, Megan! It's not like that, and no, I haven't seen your dad or brother, well not in the flesh. I've just seen their photos on your social media pages."

"Do you want to meet them too?"

"I don't know yet – I have a lot of stuff to work out in my own head and I have Alf to think about. Even though he's not my biological father, he has still been my dad for the past 35 years."

I nod, and although I'm still fuming, I remain composed.

"And what about *you*?" I turn my attention to Elliott, who is still standing quietly, like a naughty schoolboy, at Will's side.

"Will asked me to pretend to be him because he was worried you'd guess the two of you are related! Apparently, he looks a lot like Luke?"

"Yes, he does." I glance back at Will. The sun is now streaming through the arched windows of the apartment and, as shadows dance across his face masking the age difference, I could easily mistake him for Luke.

"I know I lied about that bit, but, honestly, everything else was real Megan." Elliott's eyes search mine, and the feelings return of when he kissed me in the cottage.

I nod back, silently.

"Look, should we go somewhere and talk?" asks Will, "We could maybe grab some lunch somewhere?"

I put a hand to my head, my stomach turning in disgust at the thought of food.

"I need some air," I announce, feeling suddenly very sick. Both men are at my side in an instant.

"Are you OK?" asks Will. His words seem muffled and distant.

I hear Elliott's concerned voice. "This is what happened before she blacked out the other night."

I push them off when they try to take my arms.

"I'm fine!" I say abruptly, as I stumble out of the apartment. Steadying myself against the wall, I head for the front door.

"I really think you need to sit down," says Will. I ignore him and, shrugging off his firm hold on my arm, Elliott races ahead to open the door. I'm out of the building and have almost made it to the car when I feel myself falling.

# Chapter 24

I wake to find I'm lying on the pavement next to my rental car. Elliott has my head on his knee and I can hear Will talking on the phone nearby. He ends the call when he sees I'm awake.

"That was the local doctor." Will hovers above me awkwardly, "he thinks you should head to his surgery to get checked over."

"I'm fine!" I sit up and pull my coat around me.

"I really think you should let the doctor take a look at you; you had a nasty fall!" insists Will.

"Oh really, and since when did you earn the right to give a shit?"

Will kicks an empty Coke can, which flies to the opposite side of the road, landing in the gap of a nearby drain cover.

"Suppose I asked for that," he mutters, under his breath.

"I need to get home," I say quickly. Standing shakily to my feet, I pick up Elliott's jacket from the pavement and hand it back to him without making eye contact.

"Thank you," I say, as graciously as I can manage, before pulling out the car keys from my bag. Elliott snatches the jacket and is clearly annoyed by my stubbornness. I'll be the first to admit that I'm stubborn. My dad says it's a trait I inherited from my mum; just like me, she wouldn't listen when anyone tried to tell her what to do, and she never backed down without a fight. Although I'm stubborn, I'm not a malevolent person, and I'm aware that really I should stay and talk to Will as I need to hear his side of the story. Today, however, there's just too much to take in, and even though I've figured out the truth about Will, the reality of it is now hitting me very hard.

"Please don't tell me you're thinking about driving?" questions Will angrily, as I swing open the car door. Again, I pretend to ignore him as I begin to climb into the driver's seat.

"Here Will, take my car back to the office." I watch as Elliott reaches into his pocket and throws a set of keys across the roof, motioning at a white Range Rover parked opposite the apartment. He then pulls me gently out of the way and jumps into my driver's seat.

"What the hell do you think *you're* doing?" I ask, as he buckles his seatbelt and starts the ignition.

"What does it look like?"

I look at Will, who shrugs his shoulders, then back at Elliott revving the engine, and I begin to wonder if I've met my match.

"I guess you have a chaperone then, Megan?" Will says half-smiling, before taking my arm and moving around the front of the car.

"Look after her, El," he says, guiding me into the passenger's seat. I'm too shocked to protest and silently do as I'm instructed.

"Will do, mate," answers Elliott, shifting the car into first gear. Will slams the door as Elliott pulls away.

*** 

We sit in near silence during the first half of the journey, but it's me who eventually breaks it.

"You didn't have to drive me home you know – I would have been fine," I mutter, sulkily.

"Couldn't take that risk I'm afraid, Megan." Elliott gives me a quick glance before settling his eyes back on the road. The sun is beginning to set behind the hills in the distance and, feeling shivery, I reach forward to adjust the car's heating, looking back at Elliott as I do.

"Why do you care so much?" I ask.

"You're my best mate's sister!" He answers matter-of-factly.

I bury my throbbing head in my hands. "I can't really believe this is happening."

"Well, you'd better start believing it because something tells me that Will won't just forget about you."

Elliott pauses, checks the mirror and switches on the indicator to join the motorway heading North.

"He's a good guy, Megan," he continues.

I nod back because, even though I only spoke to Will briefly, I am now beginning to feel guilty about how I reacted. Deep down, I know that Elliott is right.

I continue to gaze out of the window deep in thought and, as the miles roll by, I think about Luke. How will he feel when he finds out he has an older brother? And my dad?! How on earth will he react when he finds out he has another son? I question why Will's mother didn't tell my dad, but presume I'll never find out. Then, I think about Will again and play out our meeting earlier, which has been on a continuous loop in my mind since we left him back in Morteford. There are so many questions I want answering, but today, I just couldn't bring myself to ask them.

*** 

It feels like an eternity to get home and I'm relieved when we are finally pulling onto my street. My head is banging and I feel totally drained after the day's events.

"It's left at the end here," I say to Elliott, pointing to my house at the far end of the small cul-de-sac. I've lived in the same house for over 5 years, but never in my life have I been so relieved to see it.

"When does the car have to be back?" asks Elliott, as he pulls up outside my front gates and cuts the engine.

"I've got it for another week," I reply. "The insurance company is still dealing with a payout for mine, with it being written off, so I thought I'd keep hold of this in case I needed to go anywhere."

"Good idea," Elliott responds, looking out of the windscreen into the dark countryside beyond. *If he's hoping for a lift, he can sing for it!*

"How will you get back to Morteford?" I ask coldly. I'm still struggling with the fact that he lied to me, and even more so, that I fell for it. I've always prided myself on my foresight, and I'm disappointed that I didn't catch on sooner to his and Will's preposterous idea of switching identities.

Elliott looks at his watch, "I'll just catch the first flight back in the morning – I know a good hotel in the city centre where Will and I stay whenever we are up here on business."

I nod and open the car door. "Come in then and I'll call you a taxi."

"Thanks!"

Elliott follows me into the house and I waste no time in calling for a taxi to take him to his hotel.

"It'll be here in 15 minutes," I say, as Elliott perches on the end of the sofa and glances around.

"Nice house," he observes. His eyes scan the large living room and finally come to rest on a framed photo on the table near to him. It was taken about a year before Johnny died and we're holding hands, looking at each other longingly. Elliott realizes I'm watching him and picks up the photo, making no attempt to disguise his curiosity.

"He was a good-looking guy!" he remarks.

I cross the room, take the photo from him and, glancing at it, place it back on the table. It's obvious to me, now I look at it, that my smile is nothing but a mask to hide the fact that Johnny and I no longer had the same connection that we once shared. Anyone looking at the photo would say that we were a couple in love, with an idyllic marriage and blissful life; exactly what we wanted people to think – it was easier that way. Sometimes a photo can appear perfect because the flaws aren't instantly visible, until you pause long enough to look more closely.

"Yes, he was," I whisper.

Elliott takes another look around the room, his eyes darting back and forth as if searching for something.

"You don't have any kids?" he observes and I wonder how he knows. Although I'm aware that Elliott doesn't have children, we hadn't discussed whether Johnny and I had started a family – it's a topic I generally try to avoid. I presume his assumptions are based on the lack of family photos, and the sad absence of children's toys in my immaculately decorated, and otherwise perfect, marital home.

"No, my husband and I didn't want kids," I reply bluntly. In reality, that was only half true. For years I had longed for a family, but Johnny insisted that our lives were far too busy for children. Foolishly I'd accepted that. Looking back, maybe that's what led to me resenting him in the end; maybe a baby would have saved me, saved *us*? However, maybe not.

A short while later, Elliott's taxi appears at the bottom of the drive and he heads outside. Relieved, I follow him to the door.

"Here, take this," he says, before he leaves. He hands me an A.W.E business card showing his, and Will's, contact details.

"If you need either of us, just give us a call." He smiles and touches my arm affectionately.

Gently shrugging off his gesture, I take the card and shove it into the pocket of my jeans. I've no intention of calling either of them anytime soon.

Elliott turns to look at me hopefully as he reaches the taxi, and in return, I glare back. He nods, understanding my silent transmission, and pulls open the taxi door.

"Bye, Megan," he says, looking back one final time. Without replying, I close the door and my eyes fill with tears as the reality of today hits me with maximum force. With my back against the door, I slide down to the floor and pull my knees up to my chin.

"Bye, Elliott," I whisper, to the dark and quiet hallway.

# Chapter 25

"Are you *fucking* serious?!" Charlotte paced back and forth in front of the desk as Tony sat back and watched her anger levels rise…again!

"There's nothing we can do I'm afraid – we had to release him."

"But…we had him, didn't we?!"

"You know full well that we didn't have enough on him, and it was only a matter of time before his lawyer could get him off."

"Damn it!" Charlotte stopped pacing and whipped her hand across the desk angrily, sending a plastic holder, full of biros and highlighters, crashing to the floor. Tony bent down to clean up the mess.

"How can you be so calm, Tony? You wanted Donovan taken down again as much as I did!"

"Because I saw this coming a mile off! Remember I've had a lot more experience of him than you have. He's wriggled out of things like this countless times before so what made you think this time would be any different?"

Charlotte stamped her foot on the floor and sat down heavily in the nearest chair.

"So, he's *still* not admitting that he was driving his own car that night?"

"Nope, he's adamant that the car was stolen from his home the night of Megan's crash."

"That's just bullshit!" Charlotte growled.

"Well there's nothing we can do now. The local police are still looking for the driver of the car and, to top it off, Donovan has an alibi for that night. He was apparently at a restaurant with his wife and baby son, and a waitress can remember them. They were eating at almost the exact time that Megan says she was run off the bridge."

"Yeah, right, so, what do we do now?"

"Go home – get back to our day job. Emery and the Northumbria team will be keeping a close eye on Donovan; they have it covered here."

Charlotte nodded, although Tony knew she wasn't mellowing.

"What if he's telling the truth, Charlotte? As I said earlier, he hasn't put a foot wrong since his release from prison and he's been out a while now."

"You really believe that?" Charlotte asked, her temper fading. "That he's telling the truth and had nothing to do with Megan Cooper's car crash?"

"I think I do now, yeah." Tony said, resignedly.

Charlotte sighed loudly and rotated her neck, which was aching and stiff. A night in her own bed was more than appealing at the moment, even if her flat was a dump.

"OK then. If you *really* believe that Donovan is telling the truth, and he is innocent this time, then I'll go along with that, for now."

She stood and, after Tony had grabbed his jacket, they made their way to the door and switched off the lights.

"Time to head home, DI Taylor," Tony said, smiling. He slung his arm heavily around Charlotte's bony shoulders, a sudden spring in his step at the mere mention of 'home'. His focus was now on seeing his family, and Charlotte liked seeing him happy after the last few days.

"Yes, OK boss," she agreed, reluctantly. "Time to head home."

# Chapter 26

I'm in the bath, attempting to unwind and forget about the stresses of the day, when I get a call from DCI Morgan telling me that Rick Donovan has been released without charge. He assures me that they no longer believe he was behind the crash, and that they are back to their original suspicions. I want to believe him, but the expression in his voice forces me to read between the lines. Deep down, he thinks the same as me, that somehow, Rick Donovan is behind all of this. So, instead of feeling the reassurance intended by Morgan's phone call, I now feel terrified.

My attempts at relaxing in the bath now ruined, I escape the steamy bathroom. Wrapping myself in a towel, I pad across the landing and into my bedroom, already deciding that I'm going to call Eva and ask to stay with her and Maisie tonight. I crave the company and I really need to talk to someone about Will. I can't face telling Dad and Luke about him yet as I still need to get my own head straight before springing the news that they have a son/brother they know nothing about!

Picking up my mobile, I press Eva's number and wait anxiously for her to answer.

Her soft tone greets me, "Hi, this is Eva Cooper, please leave a message and I'll get back to you."

"Oh hi Eva, it's just me, Meg. I really need to talk to you so I'll head to yours now if that's OK; if I don't speak to you before, I'll see you when I get there. Bye."

I cancel the call and bend to switch on my bedside light, which doesn't come on. On checking the socket, and then the main light switch in the room, I realize that the power is off. This isn't unusual for our tiny housing estate, sat right in the centre of the otherwise uninhabited countryside.

"Shit!" I shout with frustration, as, with only a soft glow from the moon to assist, I am forced to feel around for some clothes. I rush to get dressed and shove the remainder into an overnight bag. Johnny and I had chosen this house on the basis that it was isolated and away from the hustle and bustle of Newcastle city centre, where we'd lived together for 3 years before deciding to relocate to the rural Northumberland setting. At times like this, I regret that decision.

Running downstairs, I tip food into Tilly's bowl and head to the garden door to call her in. I've grown to love her during the 2 years she's been with me, and she has offered me much-needed companionship at my most vulnerable of times. She was actually one of the many 'gifts' that Johnny had spoilt me with during the last couple of years of our marriage – jewellery, expensive perfume, flowers, chocolates, ornaments and pieces of art for the house; he had given it all. I'd assumed the gifts were a cover for a guilty conscience; the textbook indicator that a man has been doing something he shouldn't, plus there were the transparent lies. Even though I believed he was having an affair, by that point, the worst thing was, I didn't really care!

I'm standing in the kitchen waiting for Tilly to show up when I hear a strange sound outside. Not used to hearing many unfamiliar noises so deep into the countryside, I'm instantly alert and frozen to the spot. I glance through the half-open door, out to the far end of the garden and it's then that I see a shadow cross the blinded glass panels of the patio doors leading out to the garden beyond.

Moving slowly, I step through onto the wooden decking below. The frosty surface immediately stings my bare feet.

"Hello?"

The sound of utter silence surrounds me.

"Is there somebody out here?"

I pull my cardigan tighter around me as a small heap of fallen leaves brush against my bare ankles. The movement activates the solar security light behind me and it's then that I see her!

"No, please *please* no!"

I race down the steps leading to the lawn and towards the small mound of white fur, partially hidden under a bush. In the hazy light of the moonlight I see that she is motionless – a heavy pool of red spilling out from beneath her.

"God, no, Tilly!" I put my hand up to my mouth, stifling a scream.

The light behind me clicks off again, plunging the garden into total darkness and I feel around under the bush, trying to locate where the blood is coming from, but it's too dark. Bending to stroke her, there's still no reaction and her body feels limp. Her thick fur is cold and matted, sticky with blood. It's only when the light clicks back on that I notice a rustling in the bushes beyond my garden fence, which causes me to look upwards.

Frustratingly, the light clicks back off again and, as I adjust my vision to the darkness, the rustling continues, louder now, until it comes to a halt directly above me. A pair of eyes glint and there's a heavy, soft thud as Tilly jumps down from a nearby tree and lands right next to me, keen to check out what I'm inspecting.

"Tilly – oh thank God!" I look back down at the white ball of fluff, and on closer inspection I see it's nothing more than a stuffed toy covered in fake blood; the bright red goo that you can pick up from any supermarket at this time of year.

"Where have you been, girl?" I gasp. Relief washes over me as I pick her up and head inside. However, as I'm closing the door, I hear yet another sound from outside, and once again, the panic sets in.

Letting go of Tilly, now safely inside, I reach for a pair of plastic, summer flip-flops that I usually pop on when tending to the garden, or hanging out the washing. Another sound coming from the garden cuts through the silence. *There's definitely someone out there!*

I don't hang around long enough to find out and, even Tilly, hearing the same sound, decides to abandon her food and bounds past me for the stairs and the safety of my bedroom.

I hurry through the hall after her, not daring to directly look to the top of the stairs because, out of the corner of my eye, I can imagine the pale, lifeless shape of Johnny, willing me to stay.

"It's not real, it's not real. You're just stressed out, Meg!" I say aloud, reaching for the door and yanking it open.

Racing out into the empty street, I jump into the car, flinging my bag on the passenger's side. My heart's leaping out of my chest and from nowhere tears sting my eyes. *Was it Donovan out there? It had to be didn't it?! Does this man really want to hurt me and, if so, why?* Too many jumbled questions run through my mind.

I drive for 5 minutes until I'm safely away from home, then pull over onto the side of a quiet country lane, reaching for my phone and searching the recent call list. I press redial for DCI Morgan – it rings a few times before being picked up.

"Hello, this is Detective Constable Riley, how can I help you?" A young-sounding female answers and, thrown slightly, I try to contain my nerves before replying.

"Erm, can I speak to Chief Inspector Morgan *urgently*, please?" My voice is shaking and I take a deep breath to try and calm down.

"I'm sorry madam, DCI Morgan and DI Taylor left to travel back to Manchester earlier today. Can I help you?" she asks politely.

I'm about to respond, but hesitate.

"No, it's alright, it doesn't matter." I sigh, finally and, regaining composure, I'm suddenly aware of my overreaction; it was probably just my imagination and there was actually nobody out there. The toy covered in 'blood' was probably nothing more than a late Halloween prank; after all, the teenagers next door are known for playing tricks, and have done that type of thing before.

Rick Donovan isn't after me! I'm just tired, upset and acting a little crazy after finding out about Will. I cancel the call without any further explanation.

*** 

Within 30 minutes I'm at Eva's house and, pulling onto the drive, I don't even register that the house is empty; it's only when I reach her front door that I see that it's in complete darkness. I try the doorbell, just in case, but it's clear she isn't at home. Reaching again for my mobile, I call her, but her phone again goes straight to voicemail. Turning back to my car, there's an almighty bang, and I instinctively duck, covering my head with my hands.

The night sky lights up in an explosion of pink and green; I slowly remove my hands, standing up straight and feeling slightly pathetic! How could I forget? It's 5th November, and Eva and Maisie will be at the local annual firework display.

"Damn!" I stamp my foot against the frosty pavement, aware that I can't stand here all night. I pull my cardigan over my chest, trying to force some warmth into my body, and not savouring the thought of returning home.

I suddenly see headlights turning the corner, which pull up alongside my car on the drive. Relieved, I think at first it must be Eva, but disappointment strikes when it's not.

"Oh hi Megan, what are you doing here?" Sylvia, Eva and Johnny's mum, climbs out of the car, followed by their dad Stuart.

"Hello pet, yes, what *are* you doing here?" repeats Stuart, looking slightly surprised. He opens the back door of the car where Maisie is sitting.

"Oh, I came to see Eva." I pull my cardigan even tighter around me, aware of how I must look to my 'ex' in laws, and continue, "but she's not in!"

Sylvia looks a little confused. "We took Maisie to the firework display, but we had to cut it short because she isn't feeling very well."

I glance down at Maisie standing in the shadows, half hidden behind Stuart's left leg.

"My tummy hurts," whimpers a little voice.

"Come on little one, let's get you inside." Stuart takes Maisie's hand and then fishes in his pocket for the key to Eva's house, giving me a smile and an affectionate pat on the back as he heads for the front door.

"Hmm, so Eva's clearly not with you tonight?!" comments Sylvia, watching as her husband and granddaughter disappear inside.

"No," I answer, "I haven't seen her since Sunday when we bumped into each other at the cemetery."

"That's strange then, because she told her dad and me that she was going out with you tonight!"

"Nope, definitely not with me," I respond, feeling puzzled. There had been a few times in the past, mainly in our younger days, when I would tell a white lie to Sylvia and Stuart about Eva's whereabouts. Usually it was to cover for her meeting Steve when they first started seeing each other. Now, occasionally, she would still tell them little lies. The twins were

165

Sylvia and Stuart's only children, and now, with Johnny gone, Eva is all they have left. They've always been pretty overprotective, worrying excessively about her, but it's definitely intensified more since Johnny died.

Sylvia chuckles.

"Not to worry! No doubt she's out being wined and dined by some young man, and she didn't want to worry her dad."

I smile and nod.

"How are you anyway, Meg? Eva said you'd been in a nasty car accident and I've been meaning to call to see how you're doing?"

"Oh, I'm fine now, thanks Sylvia. You know me – made of strong stuff."

"Yes, my love, you certainly are!" Sylvia pulls her coat around her and glances towards the open door of Eva's house.

"Do you want to come inside love? You look half-frozen! Eva said she'll be back home by nine."

I look at my watch and shake my head. It's only just gone 7 pm, and I'm aware that 2 hours of pretending to Sylvia and Stuart that everything is fine is more than I'm capable of at the moment.

"Oh no thanks Sylvia, it's OK – I'd better get going. Will you tell Eva I'll give her a call tomorrow please?" I manage to retain an upbeat tone.

"Yes, will do love." Sylvia reaches out to give me a warm hug and I fight the urge to collapse into her arms. She has always been a loving and caring woman and is the closest thing I now have to a mother.

I climb back into the car and start the ignition. Pulling away from Eva's house, I have every intention of driving to Luke's flat, which is just around the corner. However, when I reach the end of the street I suddenly change my mind and, instead of turning left, turn right, heading towards the city centre.

# Chapter 27

I burst into the hotel lobby and walk quickly to the reception desk. Retrieving Elliott's business card, thankfully still in my jeans pocket, I lean against the desk and focus my attention on the girl behind it.

"Could you tell me which room Elliott Fletcher is staying in, please?" I ask, stuffing the card back in my pocket. It occurs to me that, until now, I didn't even know his surname.

The receptionist looks back at me, wide eyed. I glance down and once more pull my cardigan across my bare chest, only now aware of the fact that I forgot my bra in the rush to get out of the house. My hair's still damp and I'm clearly not appropriately dressed for the cold weather outside.

She flashes me an obviously well-practiced smile and taps on a computer keyboard in front of her.

"We do have a Mr Fletcher staying here tonight – he called to make a reservation earlier – but he hasn't checked in, sorry," she responds tightly.

I look at her, confused. Elliott left me well over an hour ago so surely he would have arrived by now?

The receptionist registers my expression and her manner softens.

"Maybe I'm wrong! I'll check the system again."

"No, it's OK, he's probably just decided to stay somewhere else," I offer, bemused.

I move away from the desk, turning full circle. Elliott definitely told me that he was staying here because he said this is the only hotel he and Will ever stay in when they visit. It's one of the most popular in the city, so why would he choose elsewhere? Alternatively, maybe he managed to catch a late flight home?

My questions are answered when I approach the revolving door and spot Elliott, standing a few metres away from the hotel and talking to a man wearing a long, dark coat, who has his back to me. They finish their conversation and, as Elliott enters the hotel, I move in front of him as he heads to the desk.

"Megan, hi! What are you doing here?" Elliott runs his fingers through his dark hair, his hand coming to a stop at the back of his neck and, at first, he appears a little awkward.

"Who was that?" I ask, curiously.

"Oh, just one of our clients – he's buying one of our places here so I thought I'd use the opportunity to catch up with him."

I nod, watching as the man disappears around a corner in the distance. Elliott looks me up and down, pausing at the bright pink flip-flops on my feet! Embarrassed I instinctively cross my arms over my chest.

"Why are you here then?" Elliott repeats, "what's wrong?"

At that moment, everything I've been trying so hard to hold together comes flooding out and I begin to sob. People passing in the lobby stare at me, intrigued, and, ignoring them, Elliott takes off his coat and wraps it around me, pulling me into a tight embrace. At first I remain rigid in his arms, but then I settle into his comforting hold and begin to relax a little.

He takes me gently by the arm, steering me next to a large marble pillar. "Wait here!" he orders. He checks in at reception and I begin to wonder what the hell I'm doing here – I really should have gone to Luke's as planned, but for reasons I don't yet want to admit, it was Elliott I wanted to see tonight.

"Do you want to come up to my room for a bit?" asks Elliott casually. Appearing in front of me, he flashes the key card, moving past me towards the lift situated at the far end of the lobby.

I pull his warm, heavy coat around me and it's only now that I realize I'm shivering. Without another word, I nod and follow him silently into the lift.

\*\*\*

His room's on the fifth floor and boasts a view of the city below. The river looks calm under the almost-full moon, and the Tyne Bridge in the distance is illuminated by the red dots of a steady flow of traffic crossing it. He switches on the bedside lamp, which instantly casts a warm glow across the room and, turning the heat to maximum, he wastes no time in heading to the mini bar and pouring us both a miniature vodka. I gratefully take the drink and perch timorously on the edge of the bed.

"You do look like you need a drink!" he remarks, standing above me. It's then that I catch a glimpse of myself in the dressing table mirror and wonder where my old, bright-eyed self has gone. My once enviable thick, long, red hair is limp and lacklustre, and my sharp, green eyes look swollen and glassy. I'm gaunt, exhausted and downtrodden and a world away from the strong and driven woman I used to be. *Is it finally time to stop being strong and, for once in my life, admit defeat?*

Unable to look at my reflection any longer, I rise from the bed and make my way to the floor-to-ceiling window. A brief flash lights the room before the sky explodes, displaying an array of brightly coloured trails behind the glass. I put one hand against the window and continue watching the impressive display as it creates multicoloured patterns across the night sky, reflecting back an identical image in the river below.

"Tell me what's wrong Megan – are you upset because of Will?" Elliott puts his empty glass on the bedside cabinet and moves to stand next to me in front of the window, waiting patiently for my answer.

"No, well, yes, but it's not just that," I whisper back, rubbing at my temples which ache from crying.

"So, tell me what it is – you can talk to me," repeats Elliott. There's another explosion as the sky comes alive again with glittering gold threads and I turn my attention to Elliott. His voice is soothing, and, just as it did the other night in the cottage, it draws me in and begs to be answered. I hesitate at first, but when I look into Elliott's eyes the words pour from my mouth and I'm rendered incapable of stopping them.

"The accident I was in – when Will saved me..."

"Yes, what about it?"

"I haven't told you the full story."

"What do you mean the full story Megan?"

"The police have been investigating and at one point they thought the driver of the other car could have been deliberately trying to force me off the road."

Elliott's blue eyes suddenly darken. "Do they know who it was?"

"Possibly. It's a man they know well, apparently."

"Do *you* know him?"

I throw back the small measure of vodka and ignore the burn as it hits my throat.

"No, I've never met him before – apparently he's just some local thug who's recently been released from prison."

"But they've got him in custody now?"

"They did have, but the detective working on the case called me tonight to tell me they had to release him, due to lack of evidence."

"So, it wasn't him then?" Elliott asks, confused.

"I don't know, but they don't think so. I'm scared Elliott! What if it was this bloke, and for some reason he wants to hurt me?"

I begin to cry, again, reduced to a whimpering mess. Never in my life have I felt so helpless and vulnerable. Even when Johnny died I managed to hold it together more than now, and it's not a feeling that sits comfortably.

"It's OK." Elliott takes my hand in his and brings his face closer to mine, forcing me to look up at him.

"I honestly don't know whether I'm coming or going, Elliott. My head is telling me that something isn't right, but the logical part of my brain is telling me to trust the police and let them do their job."

Elliott takes a tentative step forward.

"What about your heart though Megan – what's that telling you?"

I force myself to look away and laugh, awkwardly. "That's another thing altogether!"

"Listen to me – nobody is going to let anything bad happen to you. Trust me?"

I continue to weep, forcing myself to look fully into Elliott's eyes.

"Thank you." I place my other hand over Elliott's and he bends to kiss me.

His kisses are soft as he gently moves me backwards and lowers me to the bed. As he rests on top of me, I hold the back of his neck and he slips his hand under my top. His touch is warm against my still-frozen, bare skin. Suddenly he stops kissing me, inching his face away from mine and removing his hand from under my clothes, he cradles the back of my neck with his other hand.

"Are you sure this is what you want?" he asks softly.

Before answering him, I pull him towards me and kiss him tenderly on the neck, while reaching to unbutton his shirt.

"I've not felt as sure as this in a long time."

# Chapter 28

Tony was still wide awake when his phone, playing the 'Peppa Pig' theme tune, pierced the quietness of his hotel room. He reached to answer it quickly, cutting short the parting 'oink' and making a mental note to change the ring tone. He then reminded himself that he didn't have the first clue how to do it, but, unfortunately for him, his 7-year-old daughter did. On her younger brother's request she had successfully added the tune last Sunday morning, just before he received the call from Joe, asking him to come up to Newcastle. When in public, his phone was now on silent to avoid the appearance of a 41-year-old detective with a fetish for talking farm animals!

He didn't want to wake Charlotte in the room next door; she was exhausted and needed a good night's rest before they headed back to Manchester in the morning. Due to the late-night shenanigans between the couple in the room next door, he was painfully aware of how thin the walls of the hotel were.

"DCI Morgan speak—" he whispered, quietly, his voice giving up halfway through the greeting. He glanced at the clock on the muted TV in front of him; it had just gone 4 a.m. and even though he knew he hadn't slept a wink, his voice told a different story. He coughed to clear his throat, trying the seemingly difficult sentence again.

"Tony Morgan speaking," he managed, with a clearer voice.

"Tony, you sound rough did I wake you?" Joe's voice greeted him, and his was unaffected by the early hour.

"No, it's fine Joe, I was already awake. What's up?" Tony shuffled to the end of the undisturbed bed, rubbing his face with his free hand, his fingers scraping against the coarse stubble on his unshaven chin. He glanced into the mirror above the dressing table, lit only by the TV's glare in the otherwise dark room. His appearance prompted him to make another mental note – 'must have a shave in the morning before heading home'. It was a well-known fact that Liv hated a beard and, without a clean-shaven face, she wouldn't allow him anywhere near her. If he returned like this, a 'welcome home' kiss, let alone anything else, would definitely *not* be on the cards.

"You still remember where Rick Donovan lives, yeah?" asked Joe.

"Yeah, I think so. Is he still over in Jesmond?"

"Correct. Are you OK to come? I'm already there." Joe responded.

"Yes, of course – give me 15 minutes and I'll be there, but why? What's he done now?" Tony knew that anything Donovan-related would never be simple, and part of the reason he hadn't bothered going to sleep last night was because he had a foreboding that this was going to happen.

"Actually he's done nothing, for once," replied Joe. "He's dead!"

"Dead? Bloody hell – how, when?" Tony stood and reached for the TV remote to switch it off.

"He was shot at his home and his body was discovered a little while ago. I've just got here now and the CSIs are already here so I'd appreciate you coming down to take a look."

"Course, I'm on my way."

"Great, see you in a bit…oh, and Tony?" He added.

"Yeah?"

"You'd better still have a strong stomach – it's not a pretty sight!"

\*\*\*

Tony sat back in his seat and, for the second time, replayed the last loop of the CCTV footage he'd been watching. He knew what he'd watched was accurate, but he wanted to view it again, just to be certain.

The camera was positioned on the road of the hotel where he and Charlotte were staying, and it had a clear view of the whole area. It had been the final place where Donovan was spotted last night and he was now relieved that he and Charlotte hadn't headed straight home yesterday, instead choosing a well-earned rest before returning this morning.

Taking a sip of now stone-cold coffee, he placed the mug back on the desk and tried to block out the images in his head of Rick Donovan's limp and lifeless body strewn across the floor of his lounge; a large pool of blood and matter, from what remained of his skull, seeping into the cream, wool-blend carpet and spattering the light-oak furniture around him. His neighbour had discovered the body when she had woken in the night, looked out of her window and noticed Donovan's front door wide open.

Tony was grateful that Donovan's baby son had been staying with his mum at her parents' house on the night his daddy's brains were blown apart.

Forcing down another mouthful of cold coffee, purely for the caffeine hit, Tony fast forwarded the footage until he had a clear view of Donovan, captured at 7.05 pm the previous evening, entering the south end of the quayside. He continued along the street, near the hotel, keeping his head down and his coat collar turned up. It was clear that he knew he was being watched.

Two minutes later, Donovan stopped on a corner and glanced at his watch as another man arrived on the scene. The camera angle enabled Tony to get a clear image of the other man. He looked about mid-thirties with short-cropped, dark hair. He actually looked vaguely familiar, but Tony was pretty sure he'd never seen him with Donovan before.

The men had a brief conversation before it looked as though Donovan handed something to the other man which, whatever it was, he put straight into his jacket pocket. They then parted and went their separate ways. Donovan headed back along the street, exiting the same way he had entered, and Tony followed his movements until he was out of shot. The other man headed into the hotel directly behind him.

Tony picked up his mobile and hit the quick-dial menu; Charlotte answered her phone on the second ring.

"Hi Tony." She slipped on one ankle boot and began to search her room for the other. "Are you ready to head home now? I just need to finish packing my stuff and I'll meet you in the lobby, OK?"

"I'm not at the hotel, Charlotte. I'm over at the station."

"Eh, why?"

"I've been here since 5.30 am, but thought I'd let you sleep for another couple of hours as you were knackered." Charlotte was grateful for Tony's concern, however, she was also slightly annoyed that he'd gone into work without her knowledge. Tony was suddenly quiet and Charlotte heard a sharp intake of breath.

"Rick Donovan was found dead last night!"

Charlotte jumped up from the bed, stumbling over the other boot partially hidden under the mattress valance.

"Jesus Christ, where?"

"His body was found at his home over in Jesmond, in the early hours of this morning. He was shot three times before it appears he took a point-blank hit to the head."

"Any idea yet who killed him?"

"The team are looking into it now."

"Bloody hell! Have they got any suspects?"

"Possibly, yes. I've sent you through a still of CCTV footage that has just been brought to my attention. Could you do me a favour and run it past the staff on the reception desk at the hotel?"

"Yes, of course, no problem."

"The footage shows Donovan and another bloke, taken last night before he was killed. I think the other bloke could be staying in our hotel."

"OK, Tony, I'll head down to reception now and call you straight back."

Charlotte popped on her other boot and made her way towards the lobby. Racing to reception she leaned on the desk, focusing her attention on the man behind it whose badge stated he was the hotel's duty manager.

"Hi, I'm DI Taylor, Greater Manchester Police." She pulled her warrant card from her pocket, flashing it at him, then grabbed her phone from the other pocket.

"Could you tell us whether you recognize this man please? We believe he could be staying in this hotel." She accessed the photo on her phone, which Tony had sent to her. The image wasn't particularly good quality, but it was decent enough for someone to make a positive ID if they had seen him.

The man behind the desk smiled politely and removed a pair of glasses from his top shirt pocket, before scrutinizing the photo.

"Nope, sorry, can't say I've seen him," he replied. "Kerry might have done though as she was on 'til 8 pm last night." He called over a young girl in hotel uniform and slid the phone in her direction.

"Kerry, have you seen or dealt with this gentleman?" he asked. The man seemed undeterred by the questioning, but Charlotte doubted that this sort of thing happened regularly!

The girl looked flushed, providing Charlotte with the kind of reaction she was more accustomed to, and then looked down at the photo.

"Yes, I think I checked him in yesterday evening, just before I finished my shift," she replied, reasonably confidently. "We didn't have many guests check in last night."

"Can you tell me his room number please?" asked Charlotte, taking her phone and pressing redial to call Tony back, as the girl tapped into the computer.

"His name is Elliott Fletcher. Room 513," she replied, as Charlotte moved away.

"Thanks!" she shouted over her shoulder as she held the phone to her ear and waited for Tony to answer.

"Come on, Tony… pick up, for Christ's sake!" she shouted impatiently, striding quickly across the lobby. When Tony didn't answer, she cancelled the call, stuffed her phone in her pocket and headed to the lift to make her way to the fifth floor.

# Chapter 29

As I open my eyes and they gradually adjust to the grey light of the hotel room, I see that rain clouds are collecting outside. I stretch and yawn, feeling content. I hadn't slept that well in a very long time, and I can't remember the last time I felt so rested. Reaching across the king-sized bed towards Elliott, I'm greeted by an empty space and a small piece of paper, headed with the name of the hotel, resting on his pillow. I sit up and read the neat writing:

*Morning, Meg*

*Didn't want to wake you, but had to leave for first flight home. I'll call you later and arrange to meet up. I'll take you out on a real date! Really enjoyed our night together.*

*CALL ME IF YOU NEED ME!!!!!*

*EL, xxx*

Surprisingly, I'm *not* consumed by guilt, and I feel slightly ashamed for not experiencing the one emotion I imagined I *would* feel when this day finally came – the day I felt myself falling for another man. I think about Elliott; how we fell asleep in each other's arms and how, when I woke in the middle of the night, I was curled up with my back to his chest, feeling the comfort of his heartbeat. This time, thankfully, it wasn't just my imagination.

Sitting up, I stare at myself in the mirror opposite and my reflection, unlike last night, already appears less drained and washed out. I lie back on the soft pillows, replaying our night together in my mind, when there's a loud knock at the door.

A feeling of anticipation hits me. *Maybe Elliott hasn't gone back to Morteford after all?* He was worried about leaving me alone after all, although I'd insisted it'd be fine. *Maybe he's decided to stay with me today…*

I jump from the bed, quickly wrapping a sheet around me before running across the room. Swinging open the door and preparing to excitedly welcome Elliott, I'm shocked to see DI Taylor standing there.

"Oh, Inspector Taylor, hello!"

"Megan?" DI Taylor looks as confused as I feel.

"How did you know I'd be here?" I ask, feeling a little awkward about my state of undress.

"Erm, I didn't! I'm looking for an Elliott Fletcher and the reception staff told me he was staying in this room?"

Embarrassed, I explain, "I just woke up and he wasn't here – he checked out to go home." I pull the white bedsheet down onto my bare thighs, attempting to maintain the small amount of dignity I have left. "Why are you looking for him?"

"Rick Donovan has been found dead and he was spotted talking to Mr Fletcher on the corner, outside this hotel. Seems he may have been the last person he had contact with before he died."

"That was Rick Donovan?" I stagger back to the unmade bed and sit down heavily, as I fear my legs won't support me. DI Taylor follows me, uninvited, into the room.

"What… what happened to him?"

"He was shot at his home, not too far from here, last night." Taylor begins to inspect the room, stopping in front of the window to admire the view.

"He was…murdered?" I gasp. The room starts to swim and shock hits me like a strong blow to the head.

"Yes," replies Taylor calmly, before directing her attention away from the window. "Did you see Elliott Fletcher with Donovan at any point last night, Megan?"

"Maybe. I did briefly see Elliott talking to someone outside when I was waiting for him in the lobby, but the man had his back to me." I think back to the head of white hair on the other man and that I'd been able to tell by his slow movements when he walked away, that he was no longer a man in his prime.

"I had no idea that was Donovan." I say.

DI Taylor nods.

"Can you tell me how you and Elliott Fletcher know each another please?"

I fidget uncomfortably on the bed and, while DI Taylor is looking around the room, I pick up the empty condom wrapper from the bedside table and hide it in the folds of the sheet wrapped around me.

"Have you two been seeing each other long?"

"No, we only met last weekend."

DI Taylor raises her eyebrows, but something tells me she is in no position to judge!

"Do you have any idea how Elliott Fletcher and Rick Donovan are acquainted?" DI Taylor asks. "Did Elliott tell you anything about their meeting?"

"He said that he was a client of his and Will's, investing in one of the properties they're renovating – they own a property business down in Morteford." I shift my weight on the bed and wrap the sheet even tighter.

DI Taylor registers my unease and suggests that I go into the bathroom and get changed. When I return, I tell her everything; from finding the jacket, to tracking Elliott down who pretended to be Will, to me finding out that Will is actually my brother; and finally, after confronting them both in Morteford, Elliott returning me home.

Seemingly satisfied with the answers I've provided, DI Taylor leaves to update Morgan. Once again, I'm alone, questioning what, if anything, I know about my newfound brother, and the man with whom I have just spent the loveliest of nights.

# Chapter 30

"Where the hell have you been?" Charlotte flung her handbag onto the centre of Tony's desk, causing him to jump.

"Damn, sorry Char," he answered, pulling his mobile from his pocket and studying her four missed calls on the display. "I switched the bloody thing to silent again! I just figured you didn't have any luck at the hotel."

Charlotte sat down as he swung his leg over the corner of the desk and crossed his arms.

"So, any info on the guy staying at the hotel?" he asked.

"His name's Elliott Fletcher and he stayed at the hotel last night, but checked out early this morning. He had a superior room on the fifth floor." She suddenly lost her focus, "You should have seen it Tone, it was bloody huge! Panoramic views of the city, the lot. Christ, my room didn't even have a hairdryer...!"

"Taylor?"

"Sorry, sir!"

Tony returned to the first, and relevant, part of her discovery.

"What's his link to Donovan then?"

"Well, apparently, Elliott Fletcher is a property developer and he co-owns a firm down in Morteford. The company's a decent one too, if Google is anything to go by; I looked it up in the taxi on the way over here. It appears that Donovan was buying a place off them – strictly legit."

"D'you think that's true?"

"I'm not sure yet – I have the office address in Morteford, so thought we could head down there now."

"I thought you said Donovan was buying a place off him."

"I did, the company is based in Morteford, but they have a few properties up here too," she explained.

"Aah, OK." Letting out a sigh, Tony reached for his coat. He had hoped that any travelling done today would result in him seeing his family at the end of it; evidently, that was not going to be the case.

Charlotte put up her hand, stopping Tony in his tracks as he zipped up his coat.

"Hold on, that's not all."

"Go on." he responded.

"Elliott Fletcher had a guest in his room last night and, would you believe, it was Megan Cooper! That's who I got the information from, and it seems that they are on *very* close terms."

"What do you mean by very close…?"

Charlotte shook her head in dismay. For such a switched-on guy, Tony wasn't the best at reading into things of a 'romantic' nature, and she knew she would have to spell it out.

"Well Tony, put it this way – when Megan answered the door wearing nothing but a bedsheet…and a smile, as I walked in I noticed there was an empty condom wrapper on the bedside table."

Tony didn't appear as shocked as she thought he would be. It was true though that the longer you spent in this job, the easier it became to suspend disbelief.

"Did you ask her about him?"

"Yes, of course! She told me that she met him through the man who rescued her on the night of the crash."

"I thought she said she didn't know who rescued her?" Tony looked sceptical.

"She didn't at the time, but that's why she went to Morteford last weekend – to track him down. Before she handed over his jacket to us, she removed a key she'd found in the pocket; it had an address on it."

"So why didn't she tell us about it when we first questioned her?"

"She said that, at that point, she didn't realize that the crash was anything more than an accident."

"Really?"

"And, that's *still* not all! She also discovered that the man who rescued her is actually her half-brother."

"Eh, I thought she only had one brother?"

"Turns out she has a half-brother, Will Travers. He was born 5 years before Megan. Apparently, Will's mother had a brief fling with Megan's father before he settled down with Megan's mum, back here in Newcastle. Her dad doesn't even know he exists yet!"

"But this Will bloke knows?"

"Yeah, he found out just a few weeks back and decided to track Megan down on his last business visit here. He'd followed her back from work when he saw her car at the bottom of the ravine."

"Don't suppose he saw Donovan's car did he?"

"Apparently not. No."

"And he didn't stick around to see if she was OK?"

"That's what I thought, but, apparently, he didn't want her to find out they were siblings. Something to do with his dad, well the man who brought him up anyway, being on his death bed."

"This just gets weirder by the minute," said Tony.

"You're not wrong!" remarked Charlotte.

"And doesn't it all seem like one hell of a coincidence?"

"Stranger things have happened."

"Yeah, I suppose they have," he replied, picking up his car keys. "We need to get to Morteford as soon as poss. I'll call Joe from the car." Tony made his way to the exit and down to the car park. As always, Charlotte was close behind.

# Chapter 31

Will quietly closed the door to his dad's room in the care home and made his way along the corridor. Once outside, the cold air hit his flushed cheeks, but the freshness was welcoming. He thought about Alf and a lump caught in his throat – he knew his dad's time was almost up and he would never again take for granted a lungful of fresh air.

Shaking off his emotion, he made his way back to the office and was approaching the shores of Fadstow Bay, when his phone alerted him to a voicemail. Rubbing at his watery eyes, he listened to the message. Surprisingly, it was from Megan.

At first he thought maybe she'd changed her mind and wanted to meet up with him, talk properly and allow him to explain his side of the story. However, the message was to prewarn him that the police were more than likely on their way to see him and Elliott in Morteford. He couldn't catch the whole message because she was talking too quickly, but he picked up that it was something to do with the death of one of their clients in Newcastle.

Will returned the phone to his pocket and picked up his pace in the direction of the office. In truth, he really didn't have time for this today and he could feel his patience wearing thin. His poor dad was fast approaching the end of his life and his focus was purely on that. His head ached and his eyes were heavy from the tears he was trying hard to suppress; he had to be strong, not only for his mother, but for Alf too. The fact that Alf wasn't his biological father made absolutely no difference to him and now, he almost regretted trying to track down his real father, and wondered what had possessed him to track down Megan and find out where she worked/lived. It was completely out of character for him, and he could only put these ludicrous actions down to his confused state of mind at the moment. Will loved the man who had raised him as his own with all of his heart, and he was adamant that the truth wouldn't come out yet.

When the detectives pulled up outside his office Will was waiting, and he figured he would make their job easier. He knew that his office would be the first place they would go to find him and, in any case, he didn't want them knocking on his door at home and even more importantly, bothering his mum. She had enough to deal with at the moment without further stress being thrown her way.

Will wasn't at all nervous about the detectives' arrival. After all, he hadn't done anything wrong and was fully prepared to tell them the truth; he had no idea that Rick Donovan was an ex-con, and the only tie he had to them was the prospective purchase of one of their renovation properties. They had no clue about Donovan's past and obviously had nothing to do with his murder.

Elliott pulled up outside the office at pretty much the same time as the detectives. Will let out an irritated sigh and made his way to the door to greet him.

"What's going on?" asked Elliott, running to beat the detectives to the top of the steps to the office.

"I've been trying to call you!" snapped Will, keeping his voice low. "It's the police! I had a message from Megan after I'd been to see my dad this morning; she said they might be on their way."

"I was at the airport, but my phone battery was dead; I wasn't anticipating an overnight stay in Newcastle."

Will eyed Elliott suspiciously. No doubt he'd spent last night with Megan; he could tell by the pleased expression on his face! The 'love-sick puppy' spell was one he'd seen cast over Elliott many times in the 21 years that he'd known him, and although Elliott came across as ultra-confident, with a titanium exterior, the truth was that he had a sensitive soul. He'd been chewed up and spat out by more women than Will could remember. However, something told Will that this time was different. He knew very little about Megan, but from his first impressions he could tell that she wasn't the type to sleep with a guy and then break his heart; and, from the little research he'd done, he also knew that she too had been through a fair amount of heartbreak.

Will quickly dismissed the feeling of envy towards his friend. It was apparent to him that Megan was prepared to let Elliott into her life, but at the moment it seemed she had no intention of doing the same for him – even having learned that he was her own flesh and blood. He hoped, however, that she just needed time and that, perhaps in the future, she would be ready to meet. For now, he would have to get used to the idea that Megan and Elliott had something, and respect the fact that this was special to Elliott.

"Why are the police here?" whispered Elliott, as the detectives emerged from the unmarked black Insignia and made their way up the steps to join them. Will didn't get chance to explain before the two detectives stopped in front of them.

"Am I correct in thinking that you are William Travers and Elliott Fletcher?" asked the guy holding out a warrant card.

"Yes, that's right," replied Will.

"I'm Detective Chief Inspector Morgan, and this is Detective Inspector Taylor. A good-looking blonde held out her warrant card and gave Elliott an uncompromising look. In normal circumstances, she would be Will's type – petite, attractive, with a good body. She looked a few years older than him, but nevertheless, he wouldn't have said 'no'! However, just like his enthusiasm for life, his fervour for the opposite sex had also decreased over these past few months, and any sort of meaningful relationship was out of the question.

"If possible, we'd like to ask you both a few questions?" she asked, giving him a full examination.

"Look – I'm not going to lie. I already know what this is about and I can assure you that the relationship we had with Mr Donovan was purely professional and, to add, legal! He and his wife were buying a place from us, up in Newcastle, and I have all the paperwork and documentation to prove it." Will said.

"Why, anyway? Is Mr Donovan in some sort of trouble?" asked Elliott, still clueless as to what was happening.

"He's dead El," replied Will, before the detective could even answer.

"Bloody hell!" responded Elliott, open mouthed and clearly taken aback by the news. "I only saw him last night after I'd been to check on the progress of the quayside apartments. He gave me a cheque for the final payment on Number 4."

Tony studied the two men in front of him for a few seconds and then glanced at Charlotte. Catching her eye, he could tell she was thinking the same as him. Megan had clearly been in touch with her brother to alert him that they were coming to Morteford. However, it actually didn't matter that she had tipped them off and potentially given them time to get their stories straight; these two guys were innocent – absolutely no question.

"We still need to ask you both a few questions," said Tony. He knew really that he was wasting time; these two knew nothing of Donovan's true identity, but still, he had to follow protocol.

"Yes, of course." replied Will, stepping aside for them to enter the building. Elliott nodded in agreement, still in a state of perplexity.

They were on their way up the stairs and into Will's office when Charlotte's phone rang and she quickly answered it.

"Hi… yes… I understand, great, thank you very much, Anna." She ended the call and tapped Tony on the shoulder.

"Sir, can I have a word please?" They'd reached the glass doors leading into the office, where Will and Elliott stood patiently waiting for them to join them.

"Course," replied Tony, following her away from the two men and handful of staff manning the desks. Charlotte leaned against a water dispenser as Tony joined her.

"What is it?" he asked, pulling out a plastic beaker and filling it to the brim.

"That was Anna McIntyre, from forensics back in Newcastle. Emery has asked her to give us a call."

"Yeah, and...?"

"They've found the gun used to kill Rick Donovan. She's just finished testing for fingerprints on the weapon."

Tony's eyes widened. He drained the water in one and threw the empty beaker into the bin, shoving his hands in his pockets and waiting for her to continue relaying the forensic discovery.

"The gun had been dumped in a skip, not far from Donovan's property – it had been cleaned, but not well enough."

"Whose prints?"

"They found two sets – one being his own son's!"

"Connor Donovan? You think he could have killed his own father?"

"Possibly – it was no secret that the two of them didn't get on."

"He was Emery's initial suspect when we went to the crime scene this morning," admitted Tony.

"You did tell me that Connor has spent 34 years pretty much without his dad. So then when Donovan got out last time, suddenly wanting to play dad again, Connor probably resented the many years he'd already lost."

"Yes, but is that *really* a motive to kill him?"

"Maybe."

"Who did the other set of prints belong to then?" asked Tony.

"Well, this is where it becomes, shall we say, strange! The other prints apparently belong to *Johnny Cooper*!"

"What…you mean, Megan's husband? I thought he died a while ago."

"Yes, Tony," Charlotte replied, heading over to join Will and Elliott again. "He did!"

# Chapter 32

I'm more anxious than ever by the time I arrive home from the hotel. Neither Elliott or Will are answering their phones and, after leaving Will the message about the detectives' likely visit, I begin to doubt whether I should have pre-warned him. After all, I don't know Elliott that well yet, and I know even less about Will! However, I decide to follow my instinct and hope that it doesn't let me down.

Climbing out of the car and running through the torrential rain, I'm soaked by the time I've got to my front door. Shrugging off my damp cardigan, I head to the kitchen where Tilly is curled up, fast asleep on her bed. As I switch on the kettle for a hot drink, and empty food into her bowl, she stretches her limbs and lethargically makes her way over to it without a second glance.

I peer out of the window and into my rain-drenched and muddy garden. I suddenly think about Elliott and Will and wonder how they really know Rick Donovan – was he just a property investor, like Elliott said? Is it just coincidence that there's a connection between the suspect the police first thought could be behind my accident; my newly found half-brother, and the man I spent the night with?

Shivering, I turn on the central heating, moving to the living room to adjust the thermostat, and I try Elliott's phone again.

No response. The home phone's answer machine light is flashing, so I press play and prepare to receive another ear bashing from my dad, telling me that I should be resting. If only he knew the truth!

I return to the kitchen, stirring sugar into my tea when I hear a click, and a man's voice.

"Hello…Megan?"

Feeling utterly bewildered I hear my husband's voice directly behind me and I drop my cup, instantly shattering the porcelain china into dozens of pieces. The scalding fluid pools over my bare feet, but I feel nothing, I'm numb. I begin to shake uncontrollably and, frozen to the spot, am unable to turn around. I finally force myself into the hall and, although the number on the display is unknown, Johnny's voice continues to fill the room.

"Hello…look, I need to see you. Meet me at the coffee shop on Duke Street at 11.30 – see you there I hope."

I grab the phone, but the message has finished recording and the line is silent. My heart is pounding so hard that I feel dizzy. My husband is alive and, although I didn't really believe that, the fact that his body wasn't found at the time has always provided a glimmer of hope that this day would arrive. We can work things out can't we? Go back to how we were, at the beginning?

I grab my still-damp cardigan and keys. *He's alive! My husband really is alive and nothing else matters anymore…* I slide on a pair of trainers and head back out into the rain, preparing to come face to face with my husband again, and to hear the truth about what really happened that day in Spain

# Chapter 33

Elliott hesitated as he reached the corner of Jack Dalton's cottage and, tightening his hand into a fist, he banged hard, three times, on the solid, wooden door. Flecks of chipped, blue paint flaked off and drifted away into the strengthening breeze down the narrow alleyway. He stood on the doorstep for a couple of minutes, growing more and more impatient, and was just about to knock again, when the door flew open.

"Elliott! Alright mate – what you doing here?" A half-dressed Jack Dalton emerged from behind the door, squinting into the bright daylight.

"I just need a quick word." Elliott stepped forward, shadowing Jack from the sun.

"Oh yeah, sorry," replied Jack. He crossed his arms over his bare chest and pulled on the waistband of his jogging bottoms. "I was just getting some sleep – I've been working nights at the shipyard."

Elliott nodded.

"Sorry to wake you, just need to ask you something." He buried his hands deep into his coat pockets and wondered again if Megan was really in some sort of danger.

Jack rubbed his eyes and seemed to wake up slightly.

"Yeah, what is it El?"

"I was wondering if you've been in touch with Eva Cooper lately?" Elliott instantly felt awkward; although he knew Jack reasonably well from being around the same age and drinking in the same local, he didn't regard himself as a close friend, and he thought he may be overstepping the mark with such a personal question.

Jack looked instantly confused, and stayed silent.

"Eva." Elliott repeated her name in an attempt to jog Jack's memory. "You remember! The woman you met last Friday night in The Anchor, with her friend, Megan. Tall, medium length blonde hair, blue eyes?"

With no obvious sign of recognition from Jack, Elliott sighed, pulled his mobile from his coat pocket and, loading up Facebook, he brought up Megan's profile (something admittedly he'd done on numerous occasions since meeting her!). Tapping on her profile, a photo of her and Eva blinked onto his screen and he turned it to face Jack, allowing him a clear view of the girl he seemed to have very quickly forgotten about.

Still nothing – he wondered if he was still half asleep!

"You took Eva out on a date Jack!" Elliott raised his voice in frustration. "You were out *all day* together last Saturday."

Jack's confusion continued, and Elliott then began to wonder if he had the right person. However, Morteford was a tiny village and he knew that there was definitely only one Jack who fitted the description Megan had given him last Saturday, when they were in the gallery café together.

"I haven't been in the Anchor for a couple of months. Like I say, I've been working nights and unfortunately for me, that includes a Friday."

"So, you *definitely* weren't in the Anchor Tavern last Friday?"

"Nope."

"And you didn't meet a girl named Eva?"

Jack shook his head. Elliott was already mentally working out the fastest route to Newcastle at this time of day.

"Nope, and believe me, if I'd taken *her* out on a date I wouldn't forget about it that quickly," answered Jack, gazing at the photo. Elliott nodded and quickly understanding he moved away from the door. "No problem mate, and sorry to bother you."

Jack smiled before reaching to close the door. "Sorry I can't help you Elliott, but I can safely say I have never even heard the name Eva Cooper in my life."

Elliott left Jack's and, starting a slow jog back to his car, he brought up Will's number on his phone.

Will answered straight away.

"Alright, mate? Are you on your way to Newcastle yet?"

Elliott could hear the echo as Will spoke to him using hands free.

"I'm just about to leave now, so I'll be about an hour behind you."

"Great! You manage to speak to Jack Dalton yet?"

Elliott rubbed his eyes with his free hand as he rounded the corner to the car park. An icy blast of air hit his cheeks, and the coldness gripped him, causing a shiver to shoot down his spine. He was overcome by a colossal sense of unease.

"Yeah, I've just spoken to him."

"And?"

"He hasn't got a clue who Eva is, Will."

"Eh, what d'you mean? I thought he took her out last weekend?"

"Apparently not. He said he was working, and that he's never met or seen Eva before."

"But that doesn't make any sense! Why would Eva lie?"

"Your guess is as good as mine mate, but whoever Eva was with, it certainly *wasn't* Jack Dalton."

# Chapter 34

The coffee shop that Johnny suggests we meet in is where we used to go. He worked long hours most days, and a quick lunch in the café on the outskirts of Newcastle city centre was often the only chance we got to see each another properly in a 24-hour period. Some days, he would be home so late from the office that I would already be asleep, and he would have also left by the time I woke the following morning.

The coffee shop meetings were a half-hearted attempt on both our parts to spend more time together, however, closer to Johnny's death they had seemed more of a chore, and an obviously failing, last ditch attempt to save our marriage.

The rain's still falling heavily and the streets are eerily quiet. I pull onto double yellow lines, jump out of the car and run into the café, scanning it before the door is even fully open. I feel sick, but head to the counter and order a coffee before settling into a window seat and taking another look around – it's gone 11, but he isn't here.

I'm suddenly aware of my breathing and begin the fight to control the short, heavy rasps escaping from my tight chest – my heart is pounding so hard that I'm sure I'm about to collapse.

I hold the steaming cup of coffee tightly in my hand and it stings my cold fingers, the burn cutting sharply into my skin.

Instead of putting the cup down, I clench it tighter, desperate for any sort of sensation to keep a grasp on reality. I feel I'm trapped in a nightmare and am about to wake up any moment, but that doesn't happen.

I stare at my phone and the numerous missed calls from DI Taylor. I know I should call her back; it could be important, but I presume she wants to tell me what I already know, that Johnny is still alive.

The door to the café opens and then clicks shut again, a small bell chiming on its frame. I look up, preparing to see Johnny. I wonder what he'll look like; if he's aged in the 14 months since I last saw him, and if he'll think the same about me. However, it's not him, it's a middle-aged woman who catches me staring and gives me a polite nod. I fidget anxiously in my seat, and continue to wait.

Almost an hour later, still sitting in the same spot, my full mug of milky coffee is beginning to curdle and I know now that Johnny's not coming. I wonder if I should call the police, or DCI Morgan? Perhaps they could trace the call somehow and find out where he was ringing me from? Maybe he's in some sort of trouble? Although I'm confused and shocked that my husband is still alive, I'm also petrified that he is in danger or has come to harm.

Resigned, I walk towards the door, searching for my car keys, when I bang hard into someone's chest blocking my way.

"Sorry," I say, and look up to see my husband, staring straight back at me.

# Chapter 35

Tony slammed his foot on the brake, jolting Charlotte forward in her seat.

"Bloody hell Tony, you need to slow down, or you're going to kill us both before we even get to Megan!"

Tony eased off the accelerator and glanced in his rear-view mirror, where he could just make out Will Travers' car a few vehicles behind on the busy dual carriageway. The fact that the two men were now as desperate as Charlotte and him to ensure Megan's safety, only cemented the fact that they were both innocent in all of this. Travelling to Morteford today to question them in person had wasted more time and they needed to get back to the North East as quickly as possible. There was absolutely no doubt in his mind that Megan was in danger.

"Any luck?" he asked Charlotte, as she hung up her phone and rubbed at her forehead, clearly frustrated.

"They say Megan's husband, Johnny, died 14 months ago; drowned whilst on holiday in Spain with his family, but that his body was never recovered."

"Yes, we know that already."

"His sister Eva, and his 5-year-old niece, were the only people present at the time and the beach was deserted when he went missing."

"So…what are you saying?"

"Maybe he didn't die that day, but he wanted it to appear as though he did?"

"You're saying he faked his own death and managed to stay under the radar – until now?"

"Possibly."

"Why on earth would he fake his own death? Up and leave a lovely wife, a happy marriage and a beautiful home?"

"I wouldn't be so sure about the happy marriage part, Tony! Reading between the lines of what Megan told me at the hotel this morning, their marriage was as good as over when he died."

"Did she give a reason for that?"

"Not directly, no, it just seems they'd drifted apart. He was apparently spending a lot of time at work and they didn't get much chance to spend time together. I get the impression she felt like he was hiding something from her, but she wasn't sure what."

"Donovan?"

"Yes, maybe. It would certainly explain the lies and the money, and, to be honest, if I'd got on the wrong side of Rick Donovan, I think I would fake my own death!"

Tony drummed his fingers impatiently on the steering wheel.

"It just seems bizarre to me that, if Johnny had faked his own death back in Spain, why would he risk returning now?"

"Your guess is as good as mine on that one, Tony."

Tony switched on his indicator and swerved as a car narrowly missed ploughing into the side of them. He held his hand on the horn and shook his head at the other driver, who had clearly been in the wrong.

"Learn to drive, you moron!" he shouted, loudly.

"Tony, do you want me to drive?" Charlotte asked. She was witnessing another episode when he actually lost his temper, although she wasn't surprised – they were both exhausted and ready for home. Tony had clearly been looking forward to seeing Liv and the kids and, instead, he had spent the best part of the day on the road.

"Have you tried ringing Megan again?" he asked, finally relaxing slightly as the traffic began to ease.

"Yeah, still no answer – there's a couple of officers on their way to her house."

"What about Eva? Has anyone been in touch with her?"

"She's being brought in for questioning as we speak."

Tony pressed the accelerator and guided the car into the fast lane, shortly followed by Will who was now directly behind him.

"Good, now for God's sake let's get to the bottom of all this!"

# Chapter 36

Eva had been kept in the same, poky room at Newcastle police station for almost 2 hours, when the door suddenly opened and two detectives ambled in. She took a deep breath and held it, counting to 10; her whole body was shaking and the taste of her tears was beginning to sting her dry, chapped lips. The detectives introduced themselves, and she knew they had been the ones to visit Megan the day after she had arrived home from hospital.

"Miss Cooper, this is DCI Morgan, and I'm DI Taylor. We want to ask you some questions regarding Johnny and Megan Cooper."

Eva gripped the side of the table in front of her and, to prevent more tears, forced down a gulp of water from a plastic cup.

"I've already told the police everything I know," she replied defensively.

"Yes, I realize you've already been through everything, but we have a couple of things we would like to clear up," replied the female detective.

"You think my brother's still alive – don't you?" asked Eva. The thought of Johnny still being alive made her stomach flip. She'd replayed the last time she'd seen her twin brother so many times in her head that even she couldn't be sure of what really happened. One minute he was there; the next he was gone. She wasn't sure if the feelings she had were of excitement at the thought of seeing Johnny again, or the total shock of possibly finding out that he didn't drown that day.

"We're not sure if Johnny is alive," replied the male detective. "And we want you to know that the possibility is a slim one." Eva looked at the detective and managed a smile. At any other time, with an attractive man in such close proximity, she would no doubt initiate some innocent flirting, but on this occasion, she was just thankful that someone was at last being honest with her.

"Eva, we really need to find Megan." said DI Taylor, moving closer. Eva could smell her strong, flowery perfume and recognized it as one that Megan used to wear, back when she and Johnny had first got together. He always commented on how good she smelt.

"She's not at home, and she isn't answering her mobile. Can you think of anywhere at all she might be?"

"I haven't seen her since we got back from Morteford," Eva replied, feeling a stab of guilt.

"Oh! I thought you two were close?" DCI Morgan took a step forward, forcing Eva to shift back in her seat. What Megan had mentioned about him was correct; he had a very intimidating presence.

"We are close! She's my best friend."

"But you haven't seen her since your trip away together? That was almost a week ago," stated Taylor. "When precisely was the last time you saw Megan, Eva?"

"Oh, actually, she was at the cemetery – it was last Sunday afternoon after we'd got back from Morteford, and I bumped into her after she'd visited Johnny's grave."

"And you definitely haven't seen her since then?"

"No, not since Sunday."

"Have you spoken to her at all?"

Eva crossed one leg over the other, "No."

"Any reason for the lack of contact?" asked Morgan. "After all, she's been through quite an ordeal with the accident."

"I just haven't had the time," replied Eva, guiltily. "I normally text her quite a bit, but I'm in the process of getting a new phone because I lost mine while we were away. I was planning on texting her as soon as I got a new number."

The detectives remained silent causing Eva to feel even more uneasy.

"And, I've, erm, just started seeing someone."

Eva looked at the floor, feeling slightly embarrassed and extremely guilt-ridden that she had been such an inconsiderate friend of late.

"You know what it's like, when you first meet someone?" Eva focused her attention on DI Taylor, for female reassurance, which she didn't get!

"So, you've just started seeing someone…recently?" DI Taylor ignored Eva's question and glanced at Tony, before picking up a pen from the table.

"Yes," replied Eva, "We met when Megan and I were in Morteford.

"What's his name?"

"Why is that important? He has nothing to do with this."

"We'll decide about that, Miss Cooper." said Morgan, sternly.

"Do you have a photo of him?" asked Taylor, "and, we *will* need his name."

Eva shuffled uncomfortably. "Yes, just one photo, but it was taken on my old phone, the one I lost in Morteford. His name's Jack Dalton," Eva said finally. "As I said, he has nothing to do with this."

"Have you seen him since you returned home?"

"No, we were supposed to meet at a restaurant, on bonfire night, but he cancelled last minute."

"Any idea why he cancelled?" asked Taylor.

Eva shot her a cold look, her patience now really wearing thin; she was tired, confused and now worried sick about Megan.

"Something about a puncture on his way here," she answered, crossly.

"And you haven't rescheduled the date?"

"No, he said he'd call me." Eva replied. He still hadn't called, and the reality suddenly hit her of how naïve she had been. She really liked him and they'd had a fantastic time together in Morteford, but now all she cared about was Megan and Johnny; talking about Jack was wasting precious time.

"Look, you need to be searching for Megan – questioning me about my love life is not going to help find her, is it?" Eva snapped, finally losing any patience she'd been trying to retain for the last couple of hours. "Jack Dalton has nothing to do with Megan! He doesn't even know her, they didn't meet."

"I think that's where you could be wrong Miss Cooper," replied Taylor, turning on her heel and moving quickly to the door. Morgan followed and, once again, Eva was left alone in the soul-less interview room.

*\*\**

Once in the corridor, Charlotte crossed her arms and leaned against the wall.

"What do you reckon then?" she asked, searching Tony's face for answers. As always, he didn't give much away.

"I think she's smarter than she looks," replied Tony.

Charlotte nodded. She thought the same – false lashes, fake boobs, and an expensive French manicure did nothing to hide the fact that Eva Cooper was in fact, extremely bright.

Tony continued, "D'you think she's telling the truth about this Jack Dalton fella?"

"I'm not sure," replied Charlotte. "But there might be a way to find out."

Charlotte reached forward and put her hand into Tony's trouser pocket.

"Whoa there tiger – at least buy me a drink first!" He laughed.

"Oh don't panic Tony! I'm not in the business of preying on happily married men." She pulled out her hand, clutching Tony's mobile.

"What *are* you doing, Taylor?"

"Well, Tony, believe it or not, these days you can do more than just make phone calls using these things." She tapped on the screen and entered login details to Facebook.

Tony watched as she pulled up Eva's profile.

"Bloody Facebook," moaned Tony, as she scrolled through the many photos on Eva's page.

"Eva said that she'd taken a photo of Jack Dalton when they were in Morteford last weekend, and I'd be *very* surprised if she didn't post it so that her friends could see her 'new man'."

"Well well DI Taylor, you're not just a pretty face."

Charlotte stopped scrolling, her eyes widening before turning the screen to Tony.

"Am I right in thinking that *this* man is certainly not called Jack Dalton?" asked Charlotte.

Tony studied the selfie, posted last Saturday afternoon, showing Eva and a man standing on a hill overlooking Morteford. He knew straightaway who this man was as he'd seen his photo plastered in various minor case files over time and, although the crimes he'd been involved with up until now were small scale compared to his father, there was still plenty of time for that to change.

"No, that is most definitely *not* Jack Dalton," replied Tony excitedly. Already, he was striding to the station exit.

"It's Connor Donovan – Rick Donovan's son! We need to find him, and fast."

# Chapter 37

I blink rapidly, trying frantically to straighten my vision.

"Oh, sorry," I mutter to the stranger who's blocking the door, and I shuffle to one side so that he can pass.

I'm not sure now why I thought the man in front of me was Johnny, but maybe it was just wishful thinking. At first glance he looked very similar, with his thick mass of blonde hair, but as I look closer, he bears no real resemblance to Johnny at all. However, he does look vaguely familiar and I think I've seen him somewhere before, but I can't remember where. Perhaps it's work?

My despair worsens when I'm back in the car and driving home. The rain has thankfully stopped, but the ground is already starting to freeze under the prematurely darkening sky, and a white, reflective glow from the streetlamps makes the slippery surface of the pavements look mirrored.

As I accelerate away from the outskirts of the city centre, I have to remind myself that, despite my desire to rush, I need to drive carefully. I now *really* hope that Johnny is waiting for me when I get home, and images run through my head of him sitting in the living room, or at the dining table, or possibly at the bottom of the bed, next to Tilly, where I'd imagined him so many times after he'd 'apparently' died. I just hope that he's ready to talk and answer all my questions about what happened, finally putting a stop to the relentless voices inside my head. Tears form at the thought of seeing the man I once loved, however, I brush them away as my emotions suddenly turn to anger for what he's put me through.

Pulling the car onto my drive and climbing out, I notice a parked car a few metres up the road. Its engine is humming and its lights cast a spotlight on the darkening and deserted street. I fumble for my key, dropping it twice before finally managing to control my shaking hands to open the front door.

I run inside and a freezing wind gusts in behind me through the open door. After checking downstairs, I return to the hall, and my eyes rest on the top stair. *He has to be here, he just has to be.*

"Johnny!" I shout, as I run up the stairs and from room to room, "Johnny, are you here?" It's soon clear to me that he's not, but I still check the last empty bedroom, falling with disappointment onto the bed. My mind's in overdrive and all I can think about is that phone call. The anger I felt during my journey back has now diffused, and I'm growing increasingly concerned that he has actually come to some sort of harm.

I decide it's time to go to the police and I'm just about to make a move when I notice a dark stain on the rug in the middle of the floor. Rising slowly from the bed, I move over to look more closely – it's a muddy footprint and it's definitely not mine!

My heart starts thumping – nobody else comes into this room. I think back to the previous night and the noise I heard in the back garden, before I left for Eva's. *Has someone been in my house?*

I reach out to touch the mud and am shocked to find that it's still wet. *Oh my God, this has appeared while I've been waiting for Johnny – could it have been him?*

It's then I notice that the rug isn't lying exactly in the centre, where it normally is. I'm meticulous about neatness, especially when it comes to the alignment of certain household furnishings, and I slide the rug across to see a small gap in the floorboards that I'd not noticed before. Putting my finger into it, I prise the loose board away and reach down to pull out a small metal tin. On opening it, I see it's empty.

There's no doubt in my mind – this has Rick Donovan written all over it, and he, Johnny and whatever was in the tin are linked in some way. I pick it up and rush back down the stairs.

When I reach the bottom I catch sight of myself in the large hallway mirror. At first, I'm shocked – my pale features and frightened eyes stare back, and in the reflection I can see the staircase behind me, where Johnny's ghostly vision on the top step comes into focus. Pulling myself together, I drop the tin and run to the door, when another cold draught floods the hallway. This time I detect a lingering, recognizable scent – the aftershave that Will was wearing when he pulled me from the car…

# Chapter 38

As soon as Tony and Charlotte left the police station heading for their car, Will stood up from the cold wall he'd been sitting on.

"Well, what happened? Did you speak to Eva?" he asked, meeting them at the car.

"Yes," replied Tony, reaching for his keys and pulling open the driver's side door.

"And…?" Will asked expectantly.

Tony paused before climbing into the car, knowing that he shouldn't really be divulging too much information at this point. However, the concerned look on Will Travers' face confirmed how worried he was about his newfound sister's safety, and he found himself wondering how he would feel if he were in that position. He too had a younger sister and he would willingly walk over hot coals if it ensured her safety; although would he be as concerned about a sibling he'd only just met? The answer was simple – yes of course he would!

Before climbing into the car, Charlotte gave a nod to indicate that Will had a right to know the truth.

"Well?" asked Will again. He searched Tony's expression for hidden answers.

"We think we may know who ran your sister off the road that night," answered Tony.

"Does it have something to do with Eva?" asked Will.

"What makes you think that?" responded Tony.

"She lied to Megan about who she was seeing – she said he was a lad called Jack Dalton, a local from back home in Morteford, but Elliott went to see him earlier today and he's never heard of Eva."

"That's because it wasn't Jack who took her out last weekend."

"Eh? I don't follow."

"Someone was there, already aware that Eva and Megan were going to show up, and to hide his true identity, he pretended to be Jack."

"This has something to do with Rick Donovan, doesn't it?"

"Yes Will, we think that person was Rick's son, Connor."

"Connor?" questioned Will.

"Do you know him?"

"No, we've never met, but Donovan mentioned Connor a few times in conversation. He told me that he was buying the apartment back in Newcastle for him, and that he was keen to rekindle their relationship as they were no longer on friendly terms."

Tony let out a sarcastic laugh, "That's putting it lightly! I can safely say that they were most definitely *not* on friendly terms."

"It was Connor who killed Rick Donovan, wasn't it?" Just like his half-sister, Tony couldn't deny that Will was as sharp as a tack, and he was starting to realize just how alike Will and Megan were, not only in appearance.

Tony let out a deflated sigh. "We believe Connor Donovan shot his father, yes."

"Christ!" Will looked down at the icy pavement, then back at Tony.

"What does Connor want with Megan though?"

"We're not sure, but we think that her deceased husband may have had something to do with the Donovan family before he died."

Will nodded, as if he'd already figured that out. "You are going to look for Megan now, aren't you?" he asked urgently.

"Yes, of course."

"I'm coming with you then!" said Will, determinedly, and without further question he opened the back door of the car and was sitting down, seatbelt fastened, before Tony had chance to protest.

# Chapter 39

I've been in the car for about 15 minutes when I notice another vehicle is following me. Its headlights are dazzling, forcing me to slow my crawling speed down even further.

I've approached Kitley Bridge without even noticing – my mind was so preoccupied that I forgot to take the alternative route to the city centre, the route which would have diverted me away from the bridge. It's the first time I've been back here since the crash and the awful flashback floods my mind again.

The car behind me continues at a steady speed and, before I reach the bridge, I'm overcome by nerves and decide to pull over to let the other car pass. I click the indicator, and, edging as close to the bridge's barrier as I can to allow enough room, I cut the engine and wait.

The car comes into view just as my phone rings and, seeing Eva's number flash up on the screen, I instantly press the button on the hands free. At last! I was beginning to think she'd disappeared off the face of the earth.

"Eva, we need to talk!" I say eagerly, but instead of her voice, I'm greeted by a loud, harsh laugh booming through the car speakers.

"Eva?"

"No, sorry, guess again!"

"Who is this?" I ask. It's a male's voice, but not one I can recall.

"This is Jack!"

"Jack?" I'm confused at first, and rack my brains. *Do I know a Jack?* The penny then drops and I realize that maybe it's the same Jack who Eva met in Morteford – the guy she told me she was hoping to see again and who I'd suspected she'd been with on bonfire night, when I couldn't get hold of her.

"Oh, hi, Jack! Erm, we haven't met properly have we? I'm Eva's friend, Megan." I try to sound friendly, but fail miserably, really not in the mood for polite introductions today.

"I know who you are Megan!"

At that moment, the car behind me slowly pulls up alongside and I peer at the driver. Not only is he the guy who Eva met on that Friday night, at the Anchor pub, but also the person I'd bumped into, on leaving the café.

"Jack! What are you doing here?" I ask, "and where's Eva?"

He turns his head so that I can read his lips as his voice continues to echo through the car's speakers. "My guess is that she's with the police Megan, but where are you off to?"

"Home." I reply, bluntly. Eva has a tendency to attract dodgy men, and this one was no exception.

"Really? Didn't you realize you're heading in the wrong direction?" Jack points back to the road behind us.

I don't reply and I wonder how he knows where I live.

"Are you going home to see if your husband is actually there?" asks Jack sarcastically.

I glare at him through the window, my heart beating rapidly. "What do you know about my husband?" I demand.

"More than you think Megan." Jack moves Eva's phone away from his ear and holds it up to the car window. It's still in her bright pink case and he shakes it so that I can clearly see it.

"Just don't believe everything you hear…Meg."

I watch as he disconnects and lowers Eva's phone to his lap. Moments later, mine rings again, although this time, it's an unknown number. My hand shakes as I answer the call, already half suspecting what's about to happen.

"Hello…look, I need to see you. Meet me at the coffee shop on Duke Street at 11.30 – see you there I hope." Tears fill my eyes as Johnny's voice resounds around the car, and I immediately realize how naïve I've been.

I lower my head and hit my hands against the steering wheel, frustrated with my own stupidity. Of course Johnny isn't alive! This has all been some sick game by Jack Dalton, and I've played right into his hands.

The message to Eva ends and Jack's voice returns, but still nothing makes any sense. *How does Jack know Johnny?*

"I really didn't think you'd be stupid enough to fall for that Megan." Jack mocks – his face at the window again so that I can see him speak. I nod in resignation, realizing that the message on my answer machine had been a voicemail that Johnny had left for Eva a few weeks before he died, to arrange a meeting to plan their forthcoming holiday in Spain. Eva had kept the message as a reminder of her brother's voice, and obviously she still couldn't bring herself to erase it.

"What do you want Jack?" I ask. "How did you know my husband?"

"Oh I knew him, but not as well as my dad, Rick Donovan, did. You might have heard that name mentioned?"

"So, you're not Jack Dalton?" I ask, completely confused.

"No Megan, I'm not."

"You're Rick Donovan's son?"

"Got it in one! My name's Connor."

I take a few seconds to absorb this information before responding. "Well what the hell are you talking about? My husband didn't know you, or your dad." Already, I'm doubting myself.

"That's where you're wrong."

"It was you driving your dad's car that night?" I question, and although my voice is relatively calm, I feel anything but. "You forced me off the road and you nearly killed me!"

"Yes."

"But, why?" I whisper in shock.

"Because your fucking husband screwed my dad over, that's why! He's the one who tipped off the police, which resulted in my dad going to prison. Johnny's the reason I've had to spend so many years without a father."

"What does that have to do with me?"

Connor's tone is impatient.

"You're really not getting it, are you Megan? Your husband was lying all along, he wasn't who you thought he was."

"What do you mean by that – I…I don't understand?"

Connor doesn't answer; he just shakes his head angrily as the line goes dead and then he starts to reverse his car off the bridge. I restart the ignition, frightened and fully aware that I'm in danger. My hands are trembling and, as I fiddle with the gearstick trying to find first gear, my feet are shaking so much that I can't properly work the pedals. My eyes widen in horror as I peer into the rearview mirror and watch Connor stop, then hurtle towards me at high speed. *Oh, my God, he's going to push me off the bridge – not again, please, not again...*

I feel the all too familiar sensation of leaving my own body as the inside of the car begins to spin, and then, once again, everything goes black.

# Chapter 40

The air is so cold when I come round; everything is dark, my mind is blank, and there's a strange stillness, which causes me to think that maybe, this time, I am actually dead! I eventually come to my senses and realize that I'm still in the driver's seat of my car and the coldness I can feel is coming from the fully open door to my side.

A familiar pair of arms reaches across to undo my seatbelt and I'm lifted out onto the bridge.

"You're going to be OK Megan." I hear a soft voice in my ear and immediately identify it as Will's. I blink and peer further along the bridge, where Morgan and Taylor's black Insignia sits with its engine still running, the headlights casting an eerie-looking light onto the semi-frozen road of the bridge.

"Will! What are you doing here?

"What do you think? I came to make sure that my little sister is alright!" he replies, smiling. Placing me down onto my feet, he pulls me towards him in a tight, comforting hug. My body instantly stiffens at the unexpected move, but as I rest my head against his shoulder I feel much calmer.

"Thank you so much, Will." I say and move away shakily from his hold. The dark sky flashes blue as two police cars rush by on the bridge, heading down towards the woods below. It's only then that I realize that Connor Donovan's car is nowhere in sight.

"Where is he – Connor – did he get away?" I ask, moving to Will's side.

"No, he's still in his car – looks like he's unconscious." he replies. I watch through a clearing in the trees as an ambulance quickly pulls up and a paramedic makes his way to Donovan's overturned car.

"How did he end up down there? He was hurtling towards me when I fainted!"

"His brake lights came on, but he didn't slow down very much, so he must have hit black ice," replies Will. "We were behind him when it happened and I saw him go over the side."

I stare silently at the dark skid marks on the road, which disappear as a large gap opens up in the bridge's barrier. It's not far from where I had previously gone over. Another ambulance pulls up alongside and a paramedic makes her way over to us.

"Everyone OK here?" she asks me, reassuringly.

"Yes, my brother and I are fine," I respond, with relief. Will catches my eye and gives me a wink. The paramedic nods in response before heading to a police car at the far side of the bridge, where officers are busy setting up road blocks.

"It's lucky for you that Morgan and Taylor had this figured out in record time." Will points to a patrol car, where the pair are talking to other officers, before Morgan makes his way over.

"As soon as they spoke to Eva they knew that Connor Donovan was behind this," says Will.

"I take it they came to find you and Elliott in Morteford today?"

"Yeah. We honestly didn't have a clue about Rick Donovan, I hope you believe me?"

"Yes, of course I do!" I reply, adding "Is Elliott still in Morteford?"

"No, he's on his way now – he stayed behind to talk to Jack Dalton before following me here."

"The *real* Jack Dalton, you mean?"

"Yeah, the real one! The poor guy didn't have a clue what was going on when Elliott hammered on his door earlier today."

"All OK here then?" Morgan asks, in his thick Geordie accent. Taylor remains next to their car at the far side of the bridge.

"Yes, thank you so much," I say to Morgan, and hold out my hand towards him.

"No problem Megan, we're just doing our job." Morgan smiles, gripping my hand and shaking it firmly.

"I really thought my husband was still alive, but it was just Donovan's son playing a cruel game. I can't believe it was him all along."

"To be honest, we initially thought it was Johnny too."

Will's eyes flick up and he tactfully moves away so that he's out of earshot.

"Really, why?" I ask Morgan. I'm aware that now isn't the time or place that we should be having this conversation, but I'm intrigued to know the reason behind his initial suspicions.

Morgan lowers his voice. "We found the gun that was used to kill Donovan, dumped not far from where the murder took place. It had Connor's prints all over it, but it also showed traces of your husband's fingerprints too."

"So what does that prove?"

"Just that, when he was alive, Johnny had been in possession of that gun at some point. Prints remain for a long time if the item they're on is well preserved."

I nod in acknowledgement, feeling slightly nauseous at the thought of what my husband may have been involved in; however, I'm not too shocked.

"Do you know what the relationship was, between Johnny and Rick Donovan?" I ask, although I'm not convinced I want the sordid details, as, whatever it was, I'm sure it wouldn't have been good.

"We're looking into that now, but the only link they may have had was that Johnny worked in the property business, so they could have met through that. Donovan had a long list of properties on his portfolio, before he was sent to prison, and he had many people working with him. It appears that your husband was one of them. At the time, we were aware of some, but not all, of the others."

I nod, understanding.

"I'm sorry I can't tell you more, Megan. The truth is that the extent of what Johnny was involved with will probably never be known, especially now that Johnny and Donovan are both dead."

"Connor told me that Johnny tipped the police off, before his dad was locked up for the last time?" I ask.

Morgan nods as if he's already guessed as much, "I remember it well – I was the one who arrested him that night."

"So it was definitely Connor who murdered his own father?"

"Yes, he's a dangerous man, just like his father, and it was a well-known fact that the two men did not get on. We didn't realize just how dangerous Connor actually was until today and we intend to arrest him as soon as he's able to talk." Morgan's deep voice is emotionless. It's clear that there's no love lost between him and the Donovans.

I shake my head, the full force of today's sickening revelations hitting me.

"I lost track of the man Johnny was a long time before he passed away, Detective Morgan," I mutter quietly.

Morgan nods as if understanding the situation.

"Connor broke into my house today and I think he might have taken something from a tin hidden under the floorboards. Johnny must have hidden it before he died because I had no idea it was there."

"He didn't seem to be in possession of anything when we pulled him from his car, so my guess is there was money kept in that tin, which Connor must have known about."

"You're telling me that all this was about money?"

Morgan appeared slightly amused by my question, "I've seen worse done for less I'm afraid!"

I shake my head and look across at Will standing a few metres away, blowing into his hands to keep warm.

Morgan glances back behind him, where Taylor is now leaning against the bonnet of their car with her arms crossed, watching us.

"What about Connor then?"

"He's on his way to hospital now and the paramedics report he sustained some fairly bad injuries from the drop, even maybe critical."

"Oh, OK." I feel I should show more empathy towards Connor, but the guy broke into my house and tried to kill me – *twice* – so I can't feel too guilty about my lack of humanity.

"I'll keep you updated and as soon as we have any more news on Connor, I'll let you know," confirmed Morgan.

I nod my head, trying to remain strong.

Morgan notices my unease, "Really don't worry, Megan. If Connor Donovan does survive this, he'll be going to prison for a *long* time." He smiles reassuringly, says goodbye and heads back to DI Taylor, who gives me a wave before they both climb into their car and drive away.

\*\*\*

I end my call with Eva and adjust the scarf around my neck as it catches on the breeze. Folding my arms across me, I lean on the railings overlooking the river and taking a breath of icy cold air. I close my eyes and try to put the events of the last week out of my mind before going back through the revolving doors of the hotel.

I couldn't face going home tonight and, although I know I will have to do it at some point, at the moment I feel safer with

Will and Elliott in the hotel. I understand that Connor Donovan won't be coming after me again, however, that still doesn't stop me feeling apprehensive about going home. I can't rid the thought of him wandering around my house, and I do wonder if today was the first time he'd been there.

Shuddering, I try to push the image of his face to the back of my mind as I pull open the glass doors to the hotel's large bar area, and make my way over to Will; he's sitting at the window overlooking the Millennium Bridge beyond.

I pull up a chair opposite him and, as he slides a small glass containing brandy in front of me, I scrunch up my nose in disgust.

"I don't like brandy!" I say, as I push the glass away.

"Just drink it Meg, it will help with the nerves," he orders, sternly, forcing the glass into my hand. He's obviously comfortable with giving orders and is not used to 'no' – for the first time since we met, I notice how similar we are.

I do as my brother tells me, sipping the foul-tasting liquid before placing my glass back on the table.

"When's Elliott due to arrive?" I ask. Will glances at his watch and gives me a cheeky grin. I realize it's the fourth time in an hour that I've asked him that question.

"Is my company not good enough for you?" Will jokes.

"It's not that! It's been really nice chatting with you tonight Will, it's just…"

"It's alright," Will smiles. "I'm only joking and you don't need to explain." He rolls up his jumper sleeve and glances at his watch. "He should be with us any moment now," he answers, before picking up his pint of Carling and taking a quick sip.

"How are you feeling now?" he adds.

"Oh I'm OK, I think, still a bit shaken, but that's as much about discovering Johnny's secret past, as knowing Connor was trying to kill me today. It's a lot to take in!"

Will nods, "Yeah, must have been a shock to find out that the man you were married to wasn't the person you thought he was."

"I sort of knew to be honest – I just didn't want to admit it to myself at the time. I only really started questioning things once Johnny had died."

Will nods in acknowledgement. The door to the hotel bar suddenly opens and Elliott rushes in. He spots us straightaway and, within seconds, I'm in his arms.

Will clears his throat, which forces Elliott to gently pull away from me.

"Sorry mate, forgot you were there!" He smirks, pulling up a chair next to Will.

"Are you OK?" he asks, with concern. I sigh, pretty tired of people asking me the same question.

"Yes, Elliott I'm fine, well I am now anyway!" I point at Will, "Thankfully this one has a tendency to be in the right place at the right time."

"Oh yes, he's a regular guardian angel!" replies Elliott, punching his friend playfully on the arm.

"He certainly is," I agree. I take another sip of brandy and finally start to relax a little. "It was like déjà vu, him pulling me out of the car again today."

I smile at Elliott, and turn to Will, who now looks a little confused.

"How do you mean?" he asks.

"You! Lifting me from the car that night I came off the bridge, and doing it again tonight."

Will glances at Elliott, and then back to me, the confusion on his face more pronounced.

"Erm, Meg – I lifted you from the car earlier, but on the night of the crash I found you barely conscious, on the ground in the woods. I definitely didn't pull you from the car then!"

"Don't be silly!" I look first at Elliott and then at Will, waiting for one of them to laugh and admit that Will was pulling my leg; neither of them flinch. "Will?!" I let out a nervous laugh. "You reached over, undid my seatbelt, lifted me out and pulled me away from the car. You placed me on the ground while you took off your coat to put around me."

"Seriously, I'm not joking, Meg!" Will's tone turns serious. "I checked the wreckage of the car but you weren't inside and, as I was on my way back to the road, I saw you lying on the ground under a tree. I just presumed you'd managed to drag yourself out, but I promise you, I *did not* pull you from the car."

Open mouthed I stare at Will.

"But, but…you burnt your hand." I point to his left hand, still bandaged.

"No, I did this a couple of days before – caught it on a rogue piece of glass in the apartment, back in Morteford." He pulls up the dressing to reveal a deep cut in his palm.

By now I'm rendered speechless and I stare at Will, one question dominating my thoughts.

*If he really didn't pull me from the car that night, then who did?*

# Chapter 41

Connor's injuries had been severe and, after a week fighting for his life in hospital, he slipped into a coma from which he didn't wake. After hearing this information, I decided to relocate to Morteford.

I still regularly think about that night on the bridge, and I find it ironic that the same death that Connor had planned for me, resulted in his own. His car had fallen the same distance as mine, but Connor wasn't as lucky. Sometimes, I did wish I had *some* compassion, but I still feel no pity for him, and I have no real idea why he wanted me dead! I probably never will.

I did believe him though, the moment on the bridge when he told me that Johnny wasn't the man I thought he was. I can only imagine the sorts of crimes him and the Donovans were involved with.

I could probably push to find out the details of the crimes, but I really don't want to know. I was told that files on Donovan, held by the police, go back decades. At the time, although I didn't admit it, I always knew that things weren't adding up where Johnny was concerned. I never questioned where he was, what he was doing or where all the money was coming from.

A fresh start was exactly what I needed so I'd handed my notice in and now work part time in Will and Elliott's office in

Fadstow, which I love; helping them with the admin for their increasingly popular and ever-expanding business. The home I had once cherished became nothing more than an emotionless museum, housing all the things that Johnny had purchased, probably with blood money. I couldn't, and wouldn't, be part of that once I knew even a fraction of the truth.

I had far too many ghosts in my past, but a new, bright and exciting future awaits me and I can't wait!

The water of the estuary glistens under the warm summer sun as I shift my weight on the wooden bench and smile out to the water. As an elderly couple walks past and my smile widens, I hear footsteps, and a warm hand reaches from behind to touch my face.

"Your lunch, madame!" Elliott declares, as he hands me a package of freshly cooked fish and chips and sits down next to me. I kiss him on the cheek as he places a warm hand against my stomach.

"You really shouldn't be eating this sort of stuff sweetheart," he says, grinning and rubbing his hand gently across my ever-growing bump. Our first child is due in Autumn and we couldn't be happier.

Another hand reaches over to grab a chip and I playfully slap it away before Will sits down on the other side of the bench. It turns out that discovering I have another brother has been a brilliant addition to my life and, moving here to be with Elliott, has brought Will and I even closer. I honestly couldn't imagine my life without him now.

We travel back to the North East regularly to see Dad and Luke, or they sometimes come and visit us. It's lovely to see the men in my life building a natural bond which grows stronger and tighter as the time goes on.

Eva also comes over every other weekend to stay and has recently started a relationship with the *real* Jack Dalton!

Sadly, Will lost his dad, Alf, a few months ago when he finally lost his battle against the illness. Although I know he will always look at him as his real dad, and rightfully so, it's lovely to see him developing a relationship with his biological father. My dad, although shocked when he first discovered he had another son, has now fully accepted Will into the family with open arms – I always knew he would.

The three of us laugh and joke as the summer sun creeps higher into the sky and, as we chat, Elliott reaches out and takes my hand in his. I'm the happiest and most content I have ever been and am unbelievably excited about what the future will bring.

# Epilogue

In the distance, high on a hill overlooking the shimmering waters of Morteford, a man lights a cigarette and watches as the smoke rises gently into the warm, early summer air. Below him, the woman he once loved is sharing her lunch with the man she will marry, and her stomach swells with their unborn child. An inner glow shines radiantly in her eyes, something he's not seen before…

Unable to walk away, he watches her for a long time. The Donovans had discovered he was still alive and would have stopped at nothing to seek their revenge, but it's all over now. The job is done, his time is up, and he needs to move on.

Stubbing out the cigarette, he looks down at his left hand. The scars from the fire will forever be a constant reminder of her and, although over time they will fade, his memories never will. He carefully removes the gold wedding band from his finger and runs his fingertip over the carved inscription inside, gently tracing her initials alongside the ones he used to own.

He reaches into his pocket and pulls out a passport, displaying his photo and new name, along with a large sum of cash that he'd kept hidden, with a gun, in a tin under the floorboards of his old home. He knows that it won't be long until the truth is discovered and, therefore, it's time to leave her behind.

He pauses to reflect that the person he once was hadn't existed for a very long time, and he briefly wonders if that person was ever *truly* him? As so many other people do in life, he'd simply taken the wrong turn and would forever pay the price for the things he'd done.

He glances down at the small, gold ring in the palm of his hand, which had once held so many promises that, even then, he knew he would be unable to keep. It glints in the strengthening rays of the sun, the metal turning warm against his skin.

Without any hesitation, he clenches his hand into a fist, reaches behind his head and throws the ring into the water, taking one final glance down at her before reluctantly turning and walking away forever.

Pulling on a pair of shades, he soaks up the heat of the sun on his bare arms and looks forward to more of the same when he reaches his destination and a new life.

He heads quickly down the hill on the other side of the estuary, the weight upon his shoulders now starting to ease, and an appreciative smile curling at the corner of his lips.

He's almost reached his car now, parked at the bottom of the hill, when suddenly a black Insignia blocks his path. Searching for another way to pass, he suddenly resigns himself to the fact that this is it – the game's finally up. His smile fades, along with his dreams, and he silently watches as a pretty blonde woman clasping a pair of handcuffs, and a well-built man holding out a warrant card, make their steady way towards him.

# About the author

NC Marshall was born and raised in the North East of England, where she still lives with her fiancé. As a keen reader, she has always wanted to write a novel of her own and has held a dream of doing so since she was young. She enjoys travelling, and likes to get inspiration for her writing from the various places that she has been lucky enough to visit.

NC Marshall's debut novel, 'Sleep Peacefully' was listed as an Amazon UK Kindle bestseller in its categories, and reached the number 1 best-selling chart position in the 'Paranormal Suspense' genre. Her second novel 'See You Soon' was released in April 2016 and went straight into the Amazon bestseller's chart for its category. Her third novel, 'The Wrong Turn' was released in February 2017.

Thank you for reading *The Wrong Turn.* If you've enjoyed the book, it would be fantastic if you could leave a review on Amazon.

Alternatively, you can contact NC Marshall in the following ways. She would love to hear from you!

Facebook: @NCMarshallAuthor

Twitter: @nc_marshall

Email: ncmarshall15@yahoo.co.uk

# Acknowledgements

Firstly, I'd like to say a huge thanks to everyone who has read my books so far - thank you for taking the plunge with an unknown author and giving my books a try! For those who have kindly taken the time to get in touch, your comments, messages and kind words have meant more to me than you will ever know!

Big thanks to the reviewers and bloggers who have been by my side all the way, and helped to spread the word with your unwavering support and love for reading.

A massive thank you to Claire Jones, for completing the edit on *The Wrong Turn*. Your hard work, professionalism and dedication to the book has been fantastic, and I really hope that this is just the start of us working together!

Finally, thank you to my family and friends, and to my fiancé, who, as always, has been my rock, my all-important link to reality and has supported me from the very first letter.

23816309R00143

Printed in Great Britain
by Amazon